*I would like to express my special thanks
to Catherine Hapka for her help
in the writing of this book.*

"Psst—Lisa. Hey, Lisa!" Stevie Lake said in a loud stage whisper.

Lisa Atwood tore her attention away from the Moose Hill Riding Camp instructor in the center of the ring and gave her friend a questioning glance.

Stevie checked to make sure the instructor hadn't heard her. "Did you see the T-shirt Todd's wearing today?" she whispered to Lisa. "He looks pretty cute in it, don't you think?"

Lisa sighed and rolled her eyes. She should have known. "You'd better not let Phil catch you talking that way," she said with a weak smile.

"Very funny," Stevie replied. Phil Marsten was Stevie's boyfriend. The couple had met during Stevie's first stay at Moose Hill, and she had been hoping to relive a lot of romantic moments at camp this year. But for the first week, Phil had spent most of his free time hanging out with his cabin mate, Todd. Eventually she had felt so neglected that she had stopped talking to Phil for a few days, but the couple had made up. Now that she was friends with Phil again, she was friends with Todd, too. And for the past several days she had been dropping not-so-subtle hints to Lisa about how terrific he was.

The instructor, oblivious to Stevie's whispers, was still talking. "You're training your horse every time you ride him," he said. "Even if you're just going for a leisurely trail ride, the horse is learning from you all the time. His training never ends."

What he was saying was interesting, but Stevie had heard most of it before from her own riding instructor, Max Regnery, at Pine Hollow Stables. She leaned toward Lisa again. "Todd was really funny at breakfast this morning, wasn't he?" she said. "His imitation of Barry was a riot."

"Uh-huh," Lisa said, doing her best to listen to Stevie and the instructor at the same time. She *had* thought Todd's imitation of the camp director was pretty funny. That didn't mean she wanted to date him, though. She had too many other things on her mind—like paying attention in class so she could do well in the big horse show at the end of camp. It was less than two weeks away, and she knew she had a lot to learn before then.

2

Stevie opened her mouth to make another comment about Todd, but at that moment the instructor turned and looked at her. She shut her mouth and smiled innocently, while Lisa heaved a sigh of relief. Maybe now she would be able to pay attention.

Meanwhile, Carole Hanson, who was in the same riding class, hadn't heard a word of the exchange between her two best friends. For the past few days she had hardly noticed a thing besides her horse, Starlight. The big bay gelding had arrived at Moose Hill on Saturday, two days earlier. Carole had spent the first two weeks of camp riding a different horse, a skittish Appaloosa named Ditto. She and Ditto hadn't gotten along at all, but that just made her appreciate Starlight all the more now that he was here. She couldn't wait to ride him in the big show.

"It's important for you and your horse to remember that you, the rider, are in charge," the instructor told the class. "But I happen to believe it's equally important to think of everything you do as a partnership, a joint effort with each of you doing your part. In that way, you could say that riding is all about teamwork."

Carole smiled and gave Starlight a pat on the neck. The two of them definitely made a good team.

She was still thinking about that a few minutes later when class ended. As she walked Starlight around the ring to cool him down, Stevie and Lisa joined her with their own horses.

"Pretty interesting class, huh?" Carole commented.

Stevie shrugged. "I guess. But it was the same kind of stuff Max tells us all the time."

"True," Carole said. "But I think it bears repeating. Teamwork between rider and horse is important."

Suddenly Stevie's eyes lit up. She nodded vigorously, giving Lisa a sly glance. "You're right, Carole. It *is* important. So are other kinds of teamwork—between a boy and a girl, for instance."

Carole chuckled. She knew that Stevie was trying to fix up Lisa and Todd. It was obvious that Lisa wasn't interested, but that didn't stop Stevie from trying. "I don't know about that, Stevie," Carole said. "But I know what the most important kind of teamwork is—Saddle Club teamwork."

Stevie and Lisa wholeheartedly agreed with that. The three girls had formed The Saddle Club soon after Lisa had started riding at Pine Hollow. The club only had two rules: Members had to be horse-crazy, and they had to be willing to help each other with any problem, great or small.

Carole glanced at Starlight. The class hadn't been very strenuous, and he was already cooled down. "Good," she said. "Since you both agree with that, I have an important Saddle Club project for you."

"What?" Lisa asked.

Carole grinned. "To figure out how quickly we can get these horses put away so we can go to lunch. I'm starved!"

4

*　　*　　*

TWENTY MINUTES LATER the three friends left the stable and headed toward the mess hall. They cut across the large, grassy meadow that formed the center of camp. Halfway across, Stevie stumbled over a rock and almost fell.

Carole glanced back at her. "Are you all right?"

"I'm fine," Stevie said, looking around for the rock. Soon she spotted it and picked it up. "But I'd better take this and toss it in the woods so one of the horses doesn't trip on it." As she was about to turn to follow her friends, a flash of sunlight on chrome caught her eye. She shaded her eyes and gazed at a vehicle that was pulling up in front of the rec hall, which stood across the meadow from the mess hall.

"Hey, look at that," she said.

Her friends stopped and turned around. "What?" Lisa asked, squinting to see what Stevie was looking at.

Stevie pointed. "That car," she said. "Doesn't it look like the same one we've been seeing since the beginning of camp?"

"You mean the gangster car?" Carole asked with a smile. When The Saddle Club had first arrived at Moose Hill, they had seen a long, black sedan parked alongside the camp road. At the time, they had joked that the car looked as though it belonged in an old gangster film.

Lisa had spotted the car by now. She shrugged. "It does look like the same one," she said. "I wonder what it's doing back here?" The girls had seen the car again—or a very similar one—just a few days earlier. They had assumed that it belonged to the family of a camper.

Stevie was still watching as the car doors opened and several men in dark business suits climbed out. She narrowed her eyes suspiciously as the men headed into the rec hall. "I don't know," she said. "But I think it's safe to say they're not here to try out the new arts and crafts room."

"They're probably meeting with Barry about something," Carole said with a shrug. The camp director's office was in the rec hall.

"What business could Barry possibly have with people who look like that?" Stevie asked. "This is Moose Hill, not Wall Street. There's something very suspicious about all this."

Carole and Lisa exchanged glances. Stevie had a curious look in her eye. And when Stevie was curious, she didn't rest until her curiosity was satisfied—no matter how much trouble it got her into.

"I'm sure it's nothing suspicious, Stevie," Carole said quickly.

Lisa nodded. "What do we know about running a camp?" she said. "For all we know, Barry might have meetings with businessmen all the time. In fact, he probably does, since we've seen that car around so much."

"Maybe it's not even the same car," Carole suggested. "It could just be a bunch of similar-looking ones. Maybe

6

business types like their cars to match each other, just like their suits." She giggled at the thought.

But Stevie wasn't laughing. She was still gazing thoughtfully at the rec hall. "Barry has been acting awfully peculiar this year," she mused. "When you talk to him these days, he doesn't pay attention half the time. And he wasn't very sympathetic when Lisa ended up in the wrong cabin, remember?"

Lisa remembered. She had accidentally been assigned to a different cabin than her friends, and Barry hadn't tried very hard to fix the mistake. She hadn't been able to move until a few days ago. That had meant The Saddle Club had been separated for two weeks.

"So Barry's a little distracted these days," Carole said, turning and heading toward the mess hall again. "Big deal. Maybe he's not feeling well. Maybe he's in love. Or maybe he's just overwhelmed, since there are more campers this year than ever before."

"Or maybe something mysterious is going on and he's keeping it a secret," Stevie countered, her eyes bright with excitement as she walked beside her friends. "Maybe someone is blackmailing him. Or he could be mixed up in some kind of illegal horse-trading scheme."

Lisa rolled her eyes. She thought Stevie was being a bit silly, and she was quickly losing interest in the whole conversation. As far as she was concerned, camp was action-packed enough without inventing wild mysteries re-

7

volving around a car and a bunch of businessmen. "Come on, Stevie," she said. "If that car was here for something like that, do you really think it would pull right up to the rec hall in broad daylight?"

"Logical as always, Lisa," Carole said with a smile. "And right as always, too. I'm sure those businessmen are here for some totally ordinary, boring financial meeting or something."

Stevie shrugged. "Don't be too sure," she said. "Maybe it's not horse rustling, but something strange is going on around here. I've sensed it since we got here."

"Really?" Carole said skeptically. "This is the first time you've mentioned it."

"No it's not," Stevie replied as the girls reached the mess hall and paused just outside. "We saw someone mysterious in the woods that time, remember?" Carole and Stevie had heard someone or something moving away through the woods behind the cabins one evening. Stevie had thought it looked like a man in a suit, though she hadn't gotten a good enough look to be certain.

"Right," Carole said. "A very mysterious bear."

Stevie opened the door and held it for her friends. "You may not believe me now," she said, "but I'll find out what's going on around here. Just wait and see."

STEVIE WAS STILL talking about her mystery half an hour later. The Saddle Club was sitting at a table in the mess hall with Phil and Todd.

"Is she always like this?" Todd asked after Stevie had described the mysterious car for the fourth time.

"You mean completely insane?" Phil joked, helping himself to a handful of carrot sticks from the platter in the middle of the table.

Todd nodded. "Exactly."

A week earlier, Stevie would have been annoyed at Todd's comment, but now she just grinned at him. "Sure I am," she said. "It's one of Phil's favorite things about me. In fact, it's one of everybody's favorite things about me. Right, Lisa?" She turned and gave Lisa a big smile. Lisa hadn't been taking part in the conversation, and Stevie wanted to make sure she and Todd got every chance they could to talk to each other.

Lisa looked up from her plate. "What?" It was obvious she hadn't heard a word Stevie had said.

Stevie rolled her eyes. "Never mind." Suddenly she had another idea. "Hey, I was just thinking—you haven't tried out the new tennis courts yet, have you, Lisa? How about a game this afternoon after classes? It could be boys against girls." She elbowed Phil in the ribs.

"No way," Todd said quickly. "Even fantastic players like me and Phil couldn't beat all three of you at once."

"Oh." Stevie glanced at Carole. "Um, I don't think Carole wants to play. Right, Carole?"

Before Carole could answer, Lisa spoke up. "You and Carole go ahead, Stevie," she said. "I have some other things to do this afternoon."

Carole frowned. "You mean your reading list?" One of Lisa's teachers had given her a summer reading list, and Lisa had brought every single one of the books on the list to camp. She was determined to finish them all before she went home. During the first two weeks Lisa had spent so much time reading that her friends felt as though they had barely seen her. Now that they were all in the same cabin, Carole and Stevie had hoped that Lisa would spend less time on schoolwork and more time having fun with them.

"Actually, no," Lisa said. "I do have to get some reading done tonight—I'm only halfway through *Jane Eyre*—but this afternoon I was hoping to put in an extra hour or so with Major." That was the name of the horse Lisa was riding while she was at Moose Hill.

"Ugh," Todd put in. "I like riding as much as the next guy, but after a whole day of classes, it's nice to do something else for a while." He turned to Phil. "Since nobody seems to be into this tennis plan, how about you and I do some boarding before dinner?"

Stevie grimaced. As far as she was concerned, Todd's one major drawback was his obsession with skateboarding. He had brought three skateboards to Moose Hill, despite the few paved surfaces on the camp's rural grounds.

Todd noticed her expression. "Hey, Stevie, don't look so bummed out," he said. "You can borrow my spare board if you want to come with us."

"Thanks, but no thanks." Stevie sighed. "I've developed this strange fondness for my kneecaps," she said. Getting Todd and Lisa together wasn't turning out to be as easy as she had expected.

Lisa had tuned out the conversation again. She was busy planning her evening. There was a lot to accomplish, and she wanted to make sure she had time to get it all done. If she worked with Major for forty minutes after her last class and took another twenty cooling him down and putting him away, that still left half an hour before dinner for reading. Suddenly she had an idea: If she brought her book to the stable with her, maybe she could read while

11

she was cooling Major down. He was a calm horse, and she was sure he wouldn't give her any trouble if she read while they walked.

She smiled, pleased with the idea. Then the smile faded as she started to calculate how much longer it would take her to finish all the books on her reading list. The more she thought about it, the farther behind she realized she was. Camp was already more than halfway over, but Lisa was less than halfway through the twenty books on her list.

"Are you okay?" Carole's concerned voice broke into Lisa's thoughts.

Lisa saw that both Carole and Stevie were staring at her. "Of course I'm okay," she said, forcing herself to laugh a little. "Why wouldn't I be?"

Stevie shrugged. "For one thing, you haven't been listening to a word we've said. And you've barely touched your food."

Lisa picked up her fork and quickly shoveled some salad into her mouth. "I'm fine," she said through a mouthful of lettuce. "I was just thinking about what we learned in class this morning." Her friends seemed satisfied, and soon Stevie returned to her new favorite topic of conversation.

"The more I think about it, the more strange things I remember," she said. "There's the car, of course. And the mysterious figure in the woods. And have you noticed that Barry is late for things all the time now?" She nodded

12

toward the door, where the camp director was just entering.

"That proves it," Carole said sarcastically. "After all, there's no good reason why a man who's in charge of running a camp with fifty riders and a stable full of horses should ever be too busy to show up for lunch on time."

Stevie ignored the sarcasm. "Plus, he's made some pretty odd comments lately . . ."

Lisa's attention drifted back to her own thoughts. Carole might think Barry was the busiest guy around, but Lisa was sure that his schedule had nothing on her own. She poked her fork at her salad, feeling her stomach knot as she thought about everything she had to do before the end of camp. In addition to working her way through her reading list, she would have to spend a lot of time with Major practicing for the big show. There was a lot to do, and for a second Lisa wasn't sure she was going to be able to do it all. It was just too much. Then she remembered Piper.

Piper Sullivan had been Lisa's cabin mate for the first week and a half of camp. She was a tall, thin, pretty girl a couple years older than Lisa. Besides being a fantastic rider, Piper was a top student at an exclusive school and an accomplished dancer. And she made it all seem effortless, as though being perfect came naturally to her. More than anything, Lisa wanted to be exactly like that. She had always tried to do her best in everything she did. That was why she got straight As in school and why she had progressed so fast in her riding.

But lately everything Lisa had worked so hard for seemed in danger of slipping away. For the first time, she had received a less-than-perfect mark on her report card—a B+ in math. And these days it seemed she was always being reminded that as far as she had come in her riding, she still wasn't as good as Carole and Stevie. It was true that they had both been riding years longer than Lisa, but that didn't make it any easier to hear how good they were. Even worse, people usually went on to say how much Lisa was improving—implying that she still had a long way to go before she could hope to catch up to her friends. She had never been second-best at anything in her life, and she didn't particularly like the feeling now.

Piper never had to worry about things like that. What's more, she had seemed to understand Lisa's need to succeed, because she had the same need herself. Knowing that, and seeing how perfect Piper was, had been an inspiration to Lisa. She wished Piper were there now. But Piper had disappeared the week before without a word of explanation. All Barry would say was that she had been called away for personal reasons.

By this time, the conversation at the table had turned to the upcoming show. Lisa heard the words *blue ribbon* and started to listen.

Todd was grinning at Stevie. "Well?" he said expectantly. "What do you think? Will Phil win the blue ribbon in dressage, or will I?"

"Yeah, come on, Stevie," Phil urged. "Who's your pick, me or Todd?"

Stevie just shrugged and took a bite of her tuna salad sandwich. Dressage was her favorite event, and she and Belle were good at it. Phil and Todd knew that, and they knew she wanted that blue ribbon. They were just trying to get her goat, and Stevie wasn't going to give them the satisfaction. "I don't know about that," she said calmly once she had chewed and swallowed. "What I'm wondering is who's going to win the show-jumping event."

Carole's eyes lit up. "Me too," she said eagerly. "I still can't believe we're actually going to have the chance to be in it." In show jumping, the competitors had to jump a course of fences within a set amount of time. Unlike hunter jumpers, show jumpers didn't have to show perfect form or an even stride to score well. All they had to do was clear the fences any way they could. Nobody at the table had ever competed in a show-jumping event before, and everyone was sure it would be the highlight of the show.

"I know the answer to your question, Stevie," Todd said with a glance at Phil. "Barry will have to award *two* blue ribbons—one for me and one for Phil."

Carole laughed. "You know that's impossible," she said. "There's no such thing as a tie in show jumping." That was because all ties in the first round were broken by a jump-off, with a shorter course of jumps and a much shorter time limit. If more than one rider had a clean round in the jump-off, the winner was the one with the fastest time.

Todd just shrugged. "It will be the first time ever," he declared. "We'll end up with the exact same time in the jump-off, and all the rest of you will have to eat our dust."

Stevie and Carole laughed, but Lisa didn't join in. She knew Todd was just being silly, but his words still bothered her. Taking a deep breath, she asked herself, *What would Piper do?* She wouldn't pay any attention to Todd's bragging, that was for sure. She would just work that much harder until she could prove everyone wrong.

Lisa smiled a little at the thought. Just because Piper wasn't there in person anymore didn't mean she couldn't still be Lisa's inspiration. Lisa would start by working even harder to fit everything she had to do into her days, even if it meant occasionally giving up something frivolous, like going on trail rides with her friends. From now on, discipline was going to be her watchword. It would be good for her. It would make her strong, just like Piper. Instead of gossiping and giggling with her friends, she would spend more time reading. Instead of wasting time on arts and crafts and trail rides, she would work harder to get herself and Major into shape for the show. Maybe she would even start jogging. Piper had jogged every day, and she had mentioned once that the exercise cleared her mind and helped her concentrate. Lisa had always hated jogging, but that was just because she hadn't taken it seriously enough before.

For a moment she felt exhilarated by her new goals, but then she started to feel a little sad. It would be much more fun if Piper were around to share it all with. Lisa wished she knew what had happened to her friend. But Barry wouldn't tell her anything, though she had asked him over and over. She had tried to phone Piper's house at least once a day since the older girl's disappearance, but nobody ever answered. Still, she would keep trying. That was another vow she had made to herself. She wouldn't rest until she knew why Piper had left.

Meanwhile, Stevie was watching Barry, who had taken a seat with Betty, one of the senior riding instructors. The two of them were deep in conversation, and their faces were serious.

"Don't you guys think Barry looks a little pale today?" Stevie commented.

Carole glanced at the camp director. "Actually, he does look a little pale," she said. "I hope he's not coming down with something."

Stevie finished the last bite of her sandwich and pushed her plate away. "Well, whatever he's coming down with," she commented darkly, "I have the funniest feeling he caught it from those guys in the car."

"Give it up, Stevie," Todd said.

Stevie was still staring at Barry and Betty. "I wish I could read lips," she said. "I'd love to know what they're

17

talking about. They're sitting kind of close to the trash cans—maybe if I got up and just kind of strolled casually past—"

"Forget it," Carole interrupted. She crumpled her napkin and dropped it on her empty plate. "Whatever they're talking about, it's none of your business."

"It's my business if Barry is being blackmailed or something," Stevie argued. "After all, he's our friend. If he's in trouble, we ought to try to help." She paused, squinting again at Barry's mouth. She still couldn't make out a single word. "The more I think about it, the more the blackmailing theory makes sense."

"How do you figure that?" Phil asked skeptically.

"It's just a hunch right now," Stevie admitted. "But it's a *strong* hunch. And I'm sure I can prove it if I keep my eyes open for more clues."

Carole had heard enough. It was time to leave before Stevie's imagination ran away with her completely. "Come on, let's get going." She turned to Lisa and saw that her plate was still half full. "Are you almost finished? We don't want to be late for our next class."

Lisa nodded. Her stomach was still too clenched up to eat, but she didn't want her friends to know that. They would only worry about her, and she was fine. She just had a lot to do. "I'm ready when you are," she said. "I think they put something new in the tuna salad. I didn't really like it."

Just then Stevie grabbed Carole's arm. "Check it out,"

she whispered. "Barry is leaving already. What do you think that means?"

Carole rolled her eyes. "It probably means he didn't like the tuna salad either," she said. "Anyway, he's not really leaving. See? He's just standing by the door."

It was true. Barry had paused by the doorway and was slowly scanning the room. He didn't seem to be looking for anything or anyone in particular. It was more as if he was just making sure everything was in order.

"Very mysterious," Stevie commented.

Carole sighed. "Come on," she said, standing up. "Let's go."

The girls said good-bye to Phil and Todd and headed for the door. As they passed Barry, Stevie paused. She was dying to find out if her blackmail theory was correct. In books and movies, detectives were always getting people to confess with well-timed, probing questions. Maybe she could do the same thing to get Barry to reveal his troubles.

Ignoring Carole's disapproving look, Stevie walked over to Barry. "Hi," she said, trying to sound casual. "Looking for anything in particular? A little extra money to pay off some debts, for instance?"

Even Stevie couldn't have predicted Barry's reaction. "Wh-What?" he stammered. "I mean, uh, no! Not at all— nothing's wrong. Why don't you leave me alone?"

Before the surprised girls could say a word, Barry whirled and raced out the door.

3

For a moment nobody moved. Stevie recovered first. "Come on," she said. Obviously her comment had touched a nerve—she had to find out more. "We've got to follow him." Without waiting for an answer, she took off after Barry.

"Oh no," Carole said. "We have to stop her before she does something stupid." She ran out of the mess hall after Stevie.

Lisa followed. She hadn't paid much attention to Stevie's ramblings about Barry and the men in the suits, but now even she had to admit that something strange seemed to be going on. Unlike Stevie, however, she wasn't sure they should be getting involved in it—at least not until they knew what it was.

Outside, they found Stevie looking around frantically.

"He must have really been moving," she said. "There's no sign of him. Which way do you think he went?"

"I don't know," Carole said. "Maybe we should just give up and—"

"There!" Stevie interrupted. She pointed at a clump of bushes at the edge of the woods. Several branches were waving gently back and forth, even though there wasn't a hint of a breeze. "He must have gone in there."

"But there's no trail or anything," Lisa pointed out.

Stevie didn't bother to reply. She just pushed her way into the underbrush. Her friends sighed, exchanged resigned glances, and followed.

Carole and Lisa caught up to Stevie a few yards into the woods. She was peering at the ground. "It looks like there's a rough trail here, one a deer or something might use," she said without looking up. "Barry must have known it was here. He's been spending every summer here for so long that he probably knows these woods like the back of his hand. But we'll catch him." She plowed forward, and Carole and Lisa had to duck quickly to avoid being slapped by branches.

"Are you sure this is a good idea?" Carole asked, looking around nervously for poison ivy. Before lunch, she had exchanged her riding boots for sneakers with no socks, and her bare ankles felt vulnerable. "If Barry is trying this hard to get away from us, I think that's a pretty good sign that he doesn't feel like chatting right now."

"That's exactly why we have to catch him," Stevie said

as she dove under a large branch that was blocking the trail.

That didn't sound very logical to Carole, but she kept quiet. Maybe if she and Lisa just went along and kept their mouths shut, Barry would get away and Stevie would give up the chase before they were all late for class. But she knew Stevie too well to hold out much hope.

"Look!" Stevie cried, pointing down at the narrow trail ahead of her. Carole and Lisa saw a footprint in the dirt.

"That looks like a sneaker print," Lisa said. "Was Barry wearing sneakers?"

Stevie shrugged. "I didn't notice," she said. "He must have been."

Suddenly the girls heard a loud popping sound from somewhere ahead of them. "What was that?" Carole asked.

"It sounded like someone stepping on a branch," Stevie said eagerly. "We must be catching up to him. Come on!"

The woods grew thicker and more difficult to navigate as they continued down the narrow trail. At times, Lisa wasn't sure there was a trail there at all—or if there was, it must have been made by a creature no bigger than a rabbit. Stevie didn't seem to notice.

Suddenly Stevie stopped short and held up her hand. "Listen," she whispered.

Carole and Lisa listened. They didn't hear anything except insects and songbirds and the rustle of the forest going about its business. "What are we listening for?" Carole whispered at last.

"I heard voices," Stevie said, looking puzzled. "Could Barry have arranged to meet someone out here?"

"Not unless he's meeting a chipmunk," Carole said, brushing a spider off her arm with a shudder. "No sane person would come in here without a really good reason."

The girls heard a brief but unmistakable laugh coming from a few dozen yards ahead. Lisa's eyes widened. "There really is someone there," she whispered.

"Of course there is," Stevie replied. She began creeping forward at a crouch, ducking under the largest of the branches that surrounded them.

"That didn't really sound like Barry," Carole murmured to Lisa as they followed. "Besides, he didn't seem to be in a laughing mood when we last saw him, did he?"

Lisa shook her head. "I hope he's okay," she said. "I mean, what are we going to do if we find him sitting in a clearing talking to himself and laughing at his own jokes?"

Carole gulped. She was sure Stevie hadn't thought about that.

"We're almost there," Stevie hissed at them over her shoulder. "Be quiet—we don't want him to hear us and get away again."

Carole wasn't so sure about that, but she did her best to move as silently as she could.

A moment later Stevie spied a flash of blue ahead of

her. "We've got him," she breathed triumphantly. She burst through the last few feet of underbrush, emerging in a small clearing. Several boulders were scattered across the mossy ground, and a pair of figures was seated on one of the largest of the rocks, locked in an embrace. At Stevie's sudden appearance, the two gasped, parted, and leaped to their feet.

To Stevie's dismay, neither of the figures was Barry. She recognized the girl as a camper named Melissa. The boy was one of Phil's cabin mates, though Stevie couldn't remember his name at the moment. "Oh—uh—hi," she said as the two campers stared at her in astonishment.

A second later Carole and Lisa emerged behind Stevie, brushing brambles and leaves from their shirts. They were just as surprised as Stevie at the sight before them.

"What are you doing here!" the boy demanded. His expression wavered somewhere between annoyance and embarrassment. Melissa just looked embarrassed.

Stevie thought fast. "Um, we were just taking a walk," she said. "We didn't realize anyone else was out here." The excuse sounded lame, even to her. She did her best to smile nonchalantly.

The boy frowned. "Yeah, uh, so were we," he said. He grabbed Melissa's hand. "Come on, we don't want to be late for class." A moment later they were gone.

"Well, now I guess we know who made that trail," Carole said as The Saddle Club listened to the couple crashing away through the woods.

Lisa smiled. "And it wasn't a chipmunk," she said. "Or a deer."

"I don't know about that," Carole replied. "You could say it was a couple of dears. That's D-E-A-R-S."

Lisa laughed, but Stevie didn't look amused. "I can't believe we wasted all that time chasing a couple of secret smoochers," she muttered. "Meanwhile, Barry could be anywhere."

Carole glanced at her watch. "That's true, but there's only one place we're supposed to be right now," she said. "That's tacking up back at the stable. Afternoon classes start in twenty minutes."

"Uh-oh," Lisa said. "We'd better hurry." She had a flat class next, and she didn't want to miss a second of it.

As the three girls began making their way back down the tiny, twisting trail, Stevie's mood brightened a little. "He can run, but he can't hide for long," she commented. "Barry, that is. Meanwhile, that little scene we just interrupted gave me a great idea, Lisa. Why don't you and Todd go for a walk in the woods after dinner?"

Lisa sighed. "I don't think so, Stevie."

"Why not?" Stevie dodged to avoid a thornbush. "I'm sure the two of you could manage to find a nice, private little clearing of your very own." She grinned. "Maybe Melissa and what's-his-name would even share theirs."

Lisa didn't answer, but that didn't slow Stevie down one bit.

"If you and Todd get together, he'll probably get you

25

your very own skateboard for Christmas," Stevie mused. "Wouldn't that be romantic? Or better yet, maybe he'd get a skateboard built for two!"

Carole glanced back at Lisa, who was behind her on the narrow trail. Lisa's eyes were downcast, and Carole wasn't sure if it was because she was watching her step or because she was uncomfortable with the topic under discussion. It was definitely time to change the subject.

"You know, I was just thinking about the horse show," she said, interrupting whatever Stevie was starting to say about Todd's biceps. "You know how Max always makes us write down our goals before shows? I think we should do that for this show, too, even though he's not here to make us."

"That's a good idea," Lisa said, thinking of her own secret goal—to win the show-jumping competition. She knew it wasn't a goal Max would approve of. He liked them to concentrate on improving their own performance, not on competing with other riders. But Lisa didn't care.

Stevie just shrugged. "I guess we could do that," she said. "Do we have to write them down, though? I don't think I brought a single pen to camp." She gave Lisa a teasing glance. "Unlike some people, I wasn't planning to do any schoolwork here."

Lisa ignored the barb about her reading list. She was still thinking about the horse show. "I can't believe we

26

have less than two weeks left to get ready for the show," she said.

"Me either," Carole said with a grin. "I can't wait! So what do you think your goal will be, Stevie?"

"I'll have to think about it," Stevie said. "Maybe keeping Belle focused during equitation. She always concentrates when we're jumping or doing dressage, but during the easier stuff she sometimes gets distracted."

"That sounds good," Carole said, kicking a large pinecone out of her path. "What about you, Lisa?"

Lisa shrugged. She knew her friends wouldn't approve of her real goal any more than Max would. "Just to do my best, I guess," she said quietly, thinking of Piper. "My *very* best. No excuses."

Carole gave her a quick glance. Something about Lisa's expression bothered her. "Don't you want to make it something more specific?" she asked. "You said something the other day about lengthening Major's stride after a turn—how about that?"

"We'll see," Lisa said. "What about you, Carole?"

Carole suspected that Lisa was trying to take the focus off herself, but she wasn't sure why. She thought for a second as the three girls climbed over a large boulder in their path. "I think my main goal for the show will be to really concentrate on acting as a team. I'm going to try to pay even more attention than usual to how Starlight is reacting to things."

"Are you sure that's possible?" Stevie said. "You guys are such a team already that it's sometimes hard to remember you're two separate critters."

Carole smiled. "There's room for improvement in any relationship," she reminded Stevie. But she was still thinking about Lisa's goal. She opened her mouth to change the subject back to that, but Stevie spoke up first.

"Speaking of relationships," she said, "Todd told me he just broke up with his last girlfriend at the end of the school year. So this is definitely the time to snag him, Lisa—on the rebound."

Lisa just sighed again. "So, what do you think happened to Barry?" she asked quickly.

Carole couldn't help smiling a little. This time there was no question about it—Lisa was *definitely* trying to change the subject. And this time Carole couldn't blame her.

Luckily Stevie didn't suspect a thing. Todd was forgotten as soon as she started discussing the mystery.

"He must have gone the other direction coming out of the mess hall," she said. "Maybe we can track him down before class."

Carole looked at her watch again. "Not unless you've suddenly developed the power to stop time," she said. "We're going to be late as it is."

"Well, maybe after class, then," Stevie said. "After all, even you two skeptics have to admit now that something funny is going on with him."

28

"I guess so," Carole admitted. "But I'm not sure we should be interfering in it, whatever it is."

Lisa nodded. They were almost to the edge of the woods now, and she was already shifting her thoughts from Barry to her upcoming riding class. "If Barry is having some kind of personal problem, I'm sure he doesn't want us poking our noses into it."

"He would if he thought we could help him," Stevie argued. "And I'm sure we can. We're The Saddle Club, remember? Just because Barry isn't a member doesn't mean we should forget our rule about helping people."

The girls stepped out of the woods behind the mess hall. "Hold on a second," Carole said. She bent down, yanked off her sneaker, and dumped out a pebble and a small twig.

While Carole put her shoe back on, Stevie glanced around. "Hey, look," she said. "There's Barry."

Carole and Lisa looked where she was pointing. Barry was standing on a small hill near the other end of the meadow. The girls knew that the hill had a great view of the entire camp. From there you could see the entire meadow, the stables and paddocks, and most of the cabins. Even the swimming pond was partially visible through its screen of trees.

"What's he doing?" Carole asked. Even though Barry wasn't close enough to hear them, she found herself whispering.

Stevie shrugged. "It looks like he's just enjoying the view."

"He looks awfully serious, doesn't he?" Lisa said. "Kind of thoughtful. Maybe even a little sad."

"You're not going to go bother him again now, are you?" Carole asked Stevie.

"I guess not," Stevie said. As much as she wanted to find out what was going on, she didn't feel right about disturbing Barry when he looked the way he did just then. "Anyway, we have to get to class."

"Good," Carole said, turning away from Barry and going to change into her boots.

Stevie paused before following, glancing once again at the camp director. "I'm going to find out what's going on, though," she said quietly. "I won't give up until I do."

"I REALLY SHOULDN'T be doing this," Lisa said as she tightened Major's girth. It was Wednesday, and Carole and Stevie had just convinced her to come on a trail ride with them during the free hour between breakfast and their first morning classes. "I still haven't finished *Jane Eyre*." She had fallen asleep the night before trying to read the book under her covers with her flashlight. This morning the flashlight's batteries had been almost dead. Luckily her mother had packed a spare set in her suitcase.

"We're doing you a favor," Stevie replied. "All that reading can't be good for your eyes."

Lisa didn't answer. She led Major to the mounting block and swung aboard, feeling guilty about wasting this time when she could be doing something more worthwhile. Still, she didn't want to worry her friends. She knew they thought she was working too hard. And she comforted herself with the thought that she could practice lengthening and shortening Major's strides as she rode. Hadn't one of the instructors said that every ride was a learning experience for the horse?

The only thing Stevie was thinking about learning as she rode Belle toward the woods was Barry's secret. "I can't believe Barry is keeping such a low profile," she commented. "He must know we're on to him. But does he have a guilty conscience, or is he just shy?" Despite her best efforts, Stevie hadn't been able to track Barry down after classes on Monday, and he hadn't shown up for dinner. On Tuesday he had been just as scarce. He had come to lunch, but he had spent the whole time talking with Betty. There had been no chance for Stevie to talk to him alone. She had checked his office in the rec hall several times during the day, but he was never there.

As the girls rode toward one of their favorite trails, Stevie sighed. "I even thought about trying to talk to Betty about this," she said. "She and Barry are good friends. I thought she might know what's going on."

Carole looked worried. "Are you sure that's a good idea? I know they're friends, but if Barry hasn't told her what's wrong—if anything is wrong—I'm not sure it's your place to do it for him."

"It doesn't matter," Stevie said with a shrug. "Betty is so busy these days she barely has time to say hello. When I tried to start a conversation with her yesterday, she had to run off in the middle of a sentence to help Mike the stable hand with some hay bales. It almost makes me miss the days when this place had more staff than it knew what to do with."

Her friends nodded. In past years, Moose Hill had been known for its large staff, which meant that campers hardly had to lift a finger to take care of their horses. This year, The Saddle Club had arrived to find that the staff had been drastically cut, even though there were more campers and horses than ever before. The girls didn't mind a bit, since they were used to taking care of their own horses at Pine Hollow. But they knew some of the campers weren't happy about the new system.

"I haven't seen that car around since Monday, have you?" Carole asked, slowing Starlight to a walk as the trail got narrower.

"Nope," Stevie replied. "But I'm watching for it." She paused and frowned, glancing at Belle's head. The mare had both ears cocked forward as if listening to something up ahead. Stevie cocked her head to one side, listening intently. "Do you hear something?"

Carole glanced at Belle, then at Starlight, who had just cocked his own ears forward. "I don't, but it looks like they do," she said. "Don't forget, their ears are better than ours." The horses didn't seem particularly frightened, so Carole wasn't worried about encountering anything dangerous. "It's probably just another group out for a trail ride."

Lisa listened, too. "I think I hear something," she said after a moment. "It's a humming noise."

"We'd better watch out for bees," Carole said, thinking of the horses. A sting could panic them, and that could be dangerous in the forest.

Then Stevie heard it, too. "It's not that kind of hum," she said. "It sounds more like a machine or something." The girls kept quiet as they rode, listening to the sound. It grew louder with every step the horses took, and as it did, Starlight and Belle grew more nervous. Major, who was a very calm horse, didn't seem frightened, but his ears stayed pricked forward, monitoring the sound.

"It's definitely a machine—more than one, it sounds like," Carole said. She had to raise her voice to be heard over the steady thrum of motors. "Are we anywhere near a road?"

"I think there's a dirt fire road that crosses the trail up ahead," Lisa said. "But that noise doesn't sound like cars, or even a fire engine."

Just when the girls thought they would have to turn back to keep Belle and Starlight from panicking, they turned a corner on the trail and saw the source of the noise. Several bulldozers and other pieces of construction equipment were moving along the dirt road Lisa had mentioned. A white car brought up the rear of the odd parade. As the girls pulled their horses to a stop, the car pulled around the other vehicles and roared past, moving too quickly for the girls to see who was inside. Within seconds it was out of sight around a bend in the dirt road, and the sound of its motor was swallowed by the steady throb of the other vehicles' powerful engines.

Carole had to work hard to keep Starlight from bolting when the white car raced by. After a moment she managed to get the big bay gelding under control, though he continued to snort and roll his eyes nervously. Carole thought ruefully that all the teamwork in the world didn't make much difference when a car sped by only a few feet in front of a horse's nose. "What on earth is going on here?" she asked, speaking loudly to be heard above the bulldozers.

"I have no idea," Stevie said, tightening the reins to keep Belle from whirling around and racing away from the noise of the heavy machinery, which suddenly seemed louder now that they were outside the protection of the trees. "We're still on camp property, aren't we? Of course we are," she quickly answered her own question.

"They're probably just passing through," Lisa suggested. She glanced at her friends' horses. "In any case, we'd better turn back before the horses get any more upset."

"Just a second." Stevie dismounted and handed Carole her reins. "Take them back into the woods where it's quieter. I'll be there in a minute."

"Where are you going?" Carole asked.

"To find out what's going on," Stevie replied.

While Carole and Lisa took the horses back into the trees, Stevie hurried across the clearing. She yelled to the driver of the lead bulldozer, but she couldn't make herself heard over the roar of the motor. Running a safe distance ahead of the machine, she jumped into the road and waved her arms.

The driver looked startled. He brought the big machine to a stop and climbed out, leaving the motor idling. "Who are you?" he called.

Stevie hurried forward to meet him. "I'm Stevie Lake," she said. "I'm staying here at Moose Hill."

"Where?" asked the man. "Oh, you must mean that camp."

Stevie nodded. "My friends and I were out for a ride, and we heard your motors. Since we're still on camp property, we were wondering who *you* are."

"Fair question, I guess," said the man. "My name's Bill." He jerked a thumb toward the other machines, which had stopped behind his bulldozer. "The boys and I have orders to take these dozers into a field about a mile from here so they'll be ready to start clearing and building."

"Building what?" Stevie asked. "Who authorized this?"

Bill shrugged. "Don't ask me. I'm not the foreman. I just follow orders."

"Is the foreman here?" Stevie asked.

"Nope," Bill said. "You just missed him—he was in the car that just left. Now if you'll excuse me, we've got to push on."

Stevie stepped out of the road as Bill climbed back into

the bulldozer's cab and put the machine into gear. A moment later the whole line of construction equipment was on the move again.

Stevie found her friends waiting for her a short distance down the trail. "What's going on?" Carole asked as Stevie mounted.

"I don't know," Stevie said. She reported what Bill had said.

Lisa glanced at her watch. "We'd better head back," she said. "We don't want to be late."

The girls started riding back toward camp. "Do you think this is more of Moose Hill's improvements?" Carole asked. The camp had had some additions made to its grounds that year, including new cabins and tennis courts.

Stevie shook her head. "The field he was talking about must be a good three or four miles from the main part of camp," she said. "That's too far away to be building anything."

"Then what are they doing here?" Lisa asked.

"That's what I intend to find out," Stevie replied grimly.

A FEW MINUTES later the girls were knocking on the door of Barry's office. It opened and Barry peered out. "Girls?" he said. "What are you doing here? Aren't you supposed to be in your riding classes?"

"We have a few minutes before they start," Stevie replied. "Right now we need to ask you a question. What are those bulldozers doing out in the woods?"

Barry frowned. "Bulldozers? You saw bulldozers?"

Carole nodded. "They were driving down the fire road that crosses the west trails."

Barry was beginning to look angry. "I can't believe it," he muttered. "They shouldn't be there yet."

Yet? The three girls exchanged glances. What did he mean?

Barry stomped over to his desk and picked up the phone. He dialed a number, then waited, tapping his foot impatiently. He seemed to have forgotten about the girls. Stevie took that as an invitation and led the way into the office.

Finally someone on the other end of the line picked up the phone. "Hi, this is Barry from Moose Hill," Barry said. "I just heard the equipment is in the woods here already. I can't have my campers out there running into—" He stopped and listened to what the other person was saying. "I see. Well, I don't like it. I don't like it one bit. And I don't understand how a few days is going to make that much difference. The session is over in a week and a half, and then—" He paused again. "Well, all right. But they'd better not start working until the session ends and the deal is signed." With that, he slammed down the phone without saying good-bye.

Stevie waited for what she felt was a respectful amount of time. But when Barry still didn't seem to notice The

Saddle Club standing there, she cleared her throat. "Ahem. Is there something you'd like to share with us?"

Barry looked up, startled. "Oh! I forgot you were here," he said. "I guess there's no point in lying to you." He took a deep breath. "Moose Hill is being sold."

The three girls gasped. "What?" Carole cried. "What do you mean, sold? Who bought it? What are the bulldozers for?"

Barry rubbed his temples as if his head hurt. "It's kind of a long story."

Stevie sat down in one of the chairs by Barry's desk. "We have time," she said. Actually, their riding classes were starting in five minutes, but Stevie had the feeling that this story was worth being late for.

"All right." Barry waved a hand at the other chairs. "Have a seat, girls."

Carole and Lisa sat down. As she waited for Barry to begin, Carole found herself clutching the arms of the chair so hard that her fingers hurt. She forced herself to relax.

"I'll give you the worst news first," Barry said, sitting down behind his desk. "The camp—or, rather, the land it's on—is about to be sold to a development group. They're planning to knock down the camp and build a community of luxury recreational time-shares."

Even Stevie was speechless. This was a million times worse than the most outrageous of her theories had been.

Barry nodded at the horrified looks on the girls' faces. "Believe me, I know exactly how you feel," he said softly.

"I've been working here for ten years, you know. This place is my second home." He sighed. "Unfortunately, the owners aren't quite as attached to it."

"The owners?" Lisa repeated. Somehow, none of them had ever thought about who owned Moose Hill. It hadn't really seemed important—until now. "Who are they?"

"A pair of brothers, Joe and Fred Winter," Barry said. "They're getting on in years now, and they're starting to think about retiring. The camp hasn't made much of a profit lately, so it made sense for them to sell it. The trouble is, the first buyer to turn up was these developers." He sighed again. "They offered the Winters enough money to let them retire in style."

Stevie was trying to figure out what all this meant, but her brain seemed to be working in slow motion. "Couldn't they find any buyers who wanted to keep it as a camp?" she asked.

Barry shook his head. "Not for the kind of money the developers are offering. As I said, Moose Hill hasn't been a big moneymaker lately."

"But how is that possible!" Carole cried. Her knuckles were hurting again, but she hardly noticed. "It's such a wonderful place! How could it not make money?"

For the first time, Barry smiled. "I'm glad you feel that way," he said, and the girls could tell he really meant it. "Actually, there's no reason it couldn't turn a nice profit, but the brothers are really only interested in a quick fix.

It's not their only investment, and I guess they've been more involved with some of their other businesses. They forgot that this one also needed some attention. For instance, until this year they hadn't raised prices since before I got here. And the staff was getting so big there for a while that the payroll was eating up what money did come in."

"And you had to build the new stable when the barn burned down," Carole said, remembering the fire that had destroyed the old-fashioned barn that had been there on The Saddle Club's first visit to Moose Hill.

"Keeping horses here year-round for a summer-only business must be kind of expensive, too," Lisa put in.

Barry nodded. "Right on both counts," he said. "But keeping the horses year-round is one thing I wouldn't want to change. If we just rented horses while camp is in session, we wouldn't be able to guarantee their quality." He shook his head. "Still, we had to sell some of them this winter. That was tough."

"Like Basil, right?" Carole said, remembering the horse she had ridden during her first stay at camp.

Barry nodded. "Once the brothers realized we were signing up a lot of kids who were bringing their own horses this year, they decided to sell off some of our own animals."

Carole and Lisa nodded sympathetically, but Stevie was thinking about something else. "You said keeping horses year-round is one thing you wouldn't change," she said. "Does that mean there are other things you think *could* be changed—you know, to make this place more profitable?"

"Sure," Barry said. "I have lots of ideas. For instance, I think when the brothers raised the prices this year, they went a little *too* far."

"Definitely," Carole murmured ruefully. The sky-high boarding fees had been the reason she hadn't enrolled Starlight for the first two weeks.

"There are lots of things we could be doing," Barry said. "I even talked to my brother about my ideas—he's an accountant. He thinks this could be a moneymaking business." He grimaced. "Unfortunately, the brothers haven't let me implement any of the changes I suggested, even though profits have been sagging more and more every year."

Carole shook her head in amazement. She knew as well as anyone that any venture involving horses was bound to be expensive. Still, she found it hard to believe that the camp they all loved was such a financial failure.

Barry went on. "Finally, last year, the Winters went through a phase where they thought they were going to fix this place up and make it work. I had hoped that meant they would listen to my ideas. But they didn't—they just fired half the staff, then threw up a few new cabins and built some tennis courts and expected that to do the trick. I guess I was hoping it would, too. I even convinced them to run this monthlong session this year, figuring it might make a difference in the profits." He rubbed his temples again. "But when the Winters saw the numbers coming in, they decided it wasn't worth it to them anymore. All they wanted to do after that was unload the whole place, and none of my great financial ideas could change their minds."

"Maybe you should try talking to them again," Stevie urged. "You know, explain what a gold mine Moose Hill really is . . ."

"Sorry, Stevie," Barry said quietly. "It's a little late for that. The deal is almost final."

"Almost?" Stevie repeated.

Barry shrugged. "All but the final papers. Fred Winter told me they're hoping to finalize everything in the next couple of weeks. And as you saw, the new owners are eager to begin construction right away." He shook his head. "I still can't believe this place will be gone by the end of the summer."

Carole thought she saw tears in his eyes, though he managed to keep them under control. She wasn't sure she was going to be able to do the same. It didn't seem possible that Moose Hill could be closing. They had never really talked about it, but Carole had always assumed that The Saddle Club would continue to come here every summer until they went away to college—maybe even after that. Now those happy plans were ruined. It seemed so unfair.

Stevie was too upset even to think about crying. She

knew what her mystery was all about now, and she didn't like it one bit. The men in the black car had obviously been with the developers who were buying the camp. One of them had been the mysterious figure she and Carole had seen in the woods, too. And Barry's recent moodiness now made perfect sense.

Lisa was upset, too, but she felt as though she could hardly take in this new information. Her mind was already so filled with the things she had to do before the end of camp this year that she was afraid her head would explode if she started thinking about next year.

Barry stood up. "You girls had better get going," he said. "I'm afraid I've made you late for your classes. Just tell your instructors you were with me."

Stevie had almost forgotten that they were supposed to be in class. How could they even think about learning at a time like this?

Barry started to show them out of the office, then stopped them. "Listen, I'd really appreciate it if you could keep this information to yourselves," he said. "I haven't even broken the news to everybody on the staff yet, and I'd hate to ruin the campers' good time."

The Saddle Club nodded numbly. As Stevie hurried out of the rec hall with her friends, she was still having trouble thinking clearly about anything. One thought had seemingly taken over and was echoing through her mind: Could this really be the end of Moose Hill Riding Camp?

THE GIRLS MANAGED to keep Barry's secret until halfway through dinner that evening. It was easy at first—the news was so bad that for a while they hadn't even felt like discussing it with each other. But by dinnertime the shock had worn off and it seemed almost impossible *not* to talk about it. Still, they kept quiet, since Phil and Todd were sitting with them.

Once again, the boys were discussing their plans to ride away with all the ribbons at the horse show. "Okay, so if you win the blue in dressage and I win the red, who's going to take third place?" Todd asked Phil, giving Stevie a mischievous look out of the corner of his eye.

Phil shrugged and shoveled a huge bite of lasagna into his mouth. He chewed and swallowed quickly. "They'll probably just decide to retire the other ribbons, since we'll be so clearly superior to everyone else," he replied. "And I do mean *everyone*."

Stevie knew that the boys were just joking around again, but she definitely wasn't in the mood tonight. "For your information, that's not all they'll be retiring around here soon," she snapped. As soon as the words were out of her mouth, she realized what she had done. "Oops."

"Oops?" Phil said. He put down his fork and gave her a sharp look. "What do you mean, 'oops'? Spill it, Stevie."

Stevie gave Carole and Lisa a panicky glance. But Carole just shrugged. "You might as well tell them," she said. "We'll go crazy if we try to keep it to ourselves. We can trust them."

Stevie nodded, relieved. She had been dying to tell Phil the news all through the meal. After a glance around to make sure nobody else was close enough to hear, she told the two boys the whole story.

Phil and Todd were as horrified as the girls had been when they had heard the news. "We can't just sit back and let this happen!" Phil declared, waving his arms and almost knocking over his water glass.

Despite the serious topic, Stevie couldn't help smiling. It was times like this that reminded her why she liked Phil so much. "I agree," she said. "We have to find a way to save Moose Hill."

"But how?" Carole asked.

"We'll think of something," Stevie and Phil said in one voice.

Todd was shaking his head. "I don't know, guys," he said. "This whole situation sounds like some serious stuff to me. What can a bunch of kids possibly do to change it?"

"I hate to say it, but I think Todd's right," Carole said. "I'm not saying we should just give up, but I don't know if we should expect any miracles, either."

Stevie frowned. "It sounds to me like you *are* just giving up," she told Carole. She turned to Lisa. "What do you think? You're keeping pretty quiet."

Lisa looked up from her plate. She had only been half listening to the conversation. "I don't know," she said with a shrug. "Todd has a point. This is big business—and real money—we're talking about. It would be nice if we could find a way to help, but I can't imagine how. Your usual moneymaking schemes won't do it this time, Stevie."

Stevie didn't respond for a moment, and Carole gave her a surprised look. Then she saw that Stevie was glancing back and forth between Todd and Lisa with a satisfied expression on her face. Carole rolled her eyes. Even at a time like this, Stevie was obviously thrilled that Lisa had sided with Todd—even though it meant she was siding against Stevie.

Lisa was completely oblivious to Stevie's reaction. After offering her opinion, she had immediately returned to her previous activity—playing with her food and feeling guilty. That was because she had already broken her vow

47

to jog every day. In all the excitement over Barry's news, she had simply forgotten that she'd planned to go jogging during her free time after lunch. How else was she going to lose weight if she didn't exercise? And there wasn't any other time to do it today—her evening was already planned down to the minute. After dinner she had to spend an hour working with Major on lead changes. Then she was supposed to spend another hour helping Betty and some of the other campers muck out the paddocks. And she was determined to finish *Jane Eyre* that night, even if she had to stay up all night to do it.

It took an effort not to groan out loud when she thought about all the work that lay ahead of her. Jogging was definitely not an option. Still, Lisa couldn't help feeling bad. Not only was she letting herself down by not sticking to her vow, but in a weird way she felt as though she were letting Piper down, too. Piper always made time for the things she needed to do. Lisa couldn't remember how many times her cabin mate had spent her free time working with her horse, or had skipped lunch or dinner to jog or take care of other important things.

That last thought gave Lisa an idea. Since it obviously wasn't going to be easy to fit a daily jog into her already crowded schedule, maybe she could compromise a little on her vow. If she couldn't exercise to stay in shape, she would go on a diet instead—just until the show was over and she had won her blue ribbon in show jumping.

She smiled, feeling satisfied with her solution. But she

wiped the smile off her face before her friends could notice it. She didn't feel like sharing her decision with them. For one thing, they hadn't even known about her jogging vow, so they might not understand how important it was. Besides, Lisa couldn't help remembering all the times her friends had laughed about the girls at Pine Hollow who were constantly on diets. Lisa knew there was nothing wrong with dieting. After all, lots of people—including her own mother—were on diets most of the time. But she decided it would be easier to keep the whole plan a secret for now.

Since she was already compromising by substituting one vow for another, Lisa decided she wouldn't let herself compromise at all on her new diet. Luckily, she had been so lost in thought that she had only eaten a few bites of her lasagna. She pushed the rest of it aside and scrutinized the other food on her plate, deciding what she would eat.

Meanwhile, the rest of the group was still discussing Barry's news. Stevie and Phil had convinced the others that they had to make a serious effort to save the camp. "Otherwise, no matter what happens at the horse show, we'll all be losers," Stevie said dramatically.

Carole started her second helping of lasagna. "All right, then," she said. "We need to come up with a plan."

"Right," Phil said. "But I think we need some more information first. Like how much money those brothers are getting from the developers, and exactly when they're expecting the deal to be final . . ."

Stevie was already nodding. She glanced across the crowded mess hall at Barry, who was sitting with Betty at a table in the corner of the room. "I was thinking the exact same thing."

Phil grinned at her. "Great minds think alike, right?"

"Absolutely." Stevie smiled back at Phil, thinking once again how cute he was when his green eyes sparkled at her that way. That reminded her that the two of them still hadn't had much time alone together. Since they had made up after their fight, they had been so busy that they had only taken one evening stroll down to the pond—the site of their very first kiss.

"Ahem," Carole said loudly, bringing Stevie's mind back to business.

Stevie jumped up from her seat. There would be time for romance once they had saved Moose Hill. "Come on, we need to go talk to Barry. We have to find out a little more about these Winter brothers if we're going to convince them not to sell."

Carole stood up, too, but Phil stayed seated. "You go ahead," he told Stevie. "I don't think we should let Barry know that Todd and I are involved unless we have to."

"Good point," Carole said. "He might not appreciate the fact that we only managed to keep his secret for a few hours." She glanced at Lisa and noticed that her plate was still more than half full. "Hey, are you feeling okay?" she asked, suddenly concerned. "You've hardly eaten a thing."

"Sure," Lisa said. "I wasn't very hungry, that's all."

Carole stared in disbelief. "Not hungry!" she exclaimed. "After that workout we got in jump class today? You're kidding."

The others, most of whom were on their second or third helpings, also looked surprised. Lisa gulped. She had to think of a convincing response, or her secret would be out. "Um, well . . ." She forced herself to laugh. "Okay, you caught me," she said. "I had a little free time after my class this afternoon, and I went back to the cabin and pigged out on some cookies my mom packed for me." She laughed again, and this time it felt almost natural. "They were a little stale after two and a half weeks, but they still tasted awfully good. I ended up eating the whole bag."

Her friends laughed, too. "Busted!" Todd exclaimed with a grin.

Lisa felt guilty. Obviously, her friends didn't doubt her story at all. And why should they? Members of The Saddle Club didn't lie to each other. Still, she told herself, it wasn't as if this lie were hurting anybody.

"Then if you're finished, come on," Stevie said. "We've got to catch Barry before he skips out early again."

"You two go ahead," Lisa said, laying her fork and knife across the food on her plate and standing up. "You can fill me in on what he says later. I've got to . . . um . . ." She had been about to tell the truth: She wanted to get to the stable and get to work. She couldn't afford to talk to Barry for even a few minutes if she wanted to finish all her tasks for the evening.

Carole and Stevie waited expectantly. "What?" Stevie asked. "What do you have to do that's more important than saving Moose Hill?"

Lisa felt her face redden. Stevie had made it sound as though Lisa's schedule couldn't possibly be very important, and that annoyed her. What did happy-go-lucky, carefree, straight-C+ Stevie know about the kind of pressures Lisa was under?

Her anger made it easy to make her next lie sound convincing. "Actually, I'm pretty exhausted after that tough jump class and everything else today," she said. "I know it sounds silly, but I've been looking forward to a nice, cool, relaxing dip in the pond all through dinner."

"It doesn't sound silly at all," Carole said quickly, giving Stevie a dirty look. She was surprised that Lisa didn't want to come with them to talk to Barry. But Lisa had been working awfully hard since arriving at camp, and the last thing Carole wanted was to keep her from relaxing. "Go ahead. We'll fill you in later."

Stevie and Carole hurried over to Barry's table. Barry and Betty appeared to be deep in conversation, but they both looked up when the girls approached.

"Hi," Betty said. "What's up, girls?"

Stevie bit her lip. She was dying to blurt out all sorts of questions, but Barry had said that he hadn't told all the staff yet about the camp's sale. What if Betty was among those who didn't know? "Um, so, Barry," she said, trying her best to sound casual, "Carole and I were just thinking

52

about what you were saying this morning, about . . .
um . . ."

Barry came to her rescue. "Don't worry, Stevie," he
said. "You can speak freely. Betty knows all about it. She
was the first one I told—she's been here as long as I have."

Betty nodded. "Ten years," she said quietly. "Some of
the others on the staff have been here almost as long."
She shrugged dejectedly. "I don't know what we're all
going to do when this place closes."

"Maybe we should open our own camp someplace
where the real estate isn't quite so valuable," Barry said
jokingly.

Stevie pulled up a chair. "Don't start shopping for that
land yet," she said in a businesslike voice. "Nothing's final
until the papers are signed." She had picked up that
phrase from her parents, who were both lawyers. "First of
all, we've got to know more about the Winter brothers."

"I appreciate what you're trying to do, Stevie," Barry
said. "But I'm afraid there's really no point. Moose Hill is
gone. I'm finally starting to accept it. You're going to have
to do the same."

Carole sat down next to Stevie. "We know that, Barry,"
she said soothingly. "We're just curious, that's all."

Stevie shot her a dirty look, but her expression brightened when Barry and Betty glanced at each other and
shrugged. She realized that Carole wasn't really giving
up—she was just trying to get the adults talking.

"I don't blame you for being curious," Betty said. "It's

53

hard to believe that something like this could happen to such a great place."

Barry nodded. "I don't want you to get the wrong idea about the Winters," he said. "They're not bad guys. In fact, they've been awfully good to the staff here—they even found jobs at their other businesses for some of the people they fired this year. And they took a lot of pride in the reputation we've built over the years. Unfortunately, that's not as important to them at this point as cold, hard cash."

"It's too bad that these developers happened along and were willing to pay so much," Betty put in. "There wasn't much chance that anyone who wasn't familiar with Moose Hill would want to invest that heavily in a riding camp. But that's just because the camp's real potential hasn't been brought out."

That gave Stevie a great idea. "I've got it!" she cried, turning to Barry. "Why don't *you* buy it? You know all about the potential, and you said your brother was advising you about the money part—"

Barry cut her off with a rueful smile. "I'm way ahead of you on that one, Stevie," he said. "It was the first thing I thought of when I heard that the brothers wanted to sell. But the developers' offer is just too high."

"Are you sure?" Carole asked. "Maybe you could get a big loan from the bank or something."

"Believe me, I'm sure," Barry said with a heavy sigh. "I've been over the numbers a hundred times. Even with the biggest bank loan I could get, along with my savings and an optimistic estimate of what I could beg, borrow, or steal from family and friends, I'm still a good thirty thousand dollars short."

Stevie and Carole couldn't help gasping at the number. "Th-Thirty thousand?" Carole repeated in disbelief.

Barry nodded. "It's a shame, too. I'm sure the brothers would break off negotiations with the developers if they thought I could match their price."

"I'm sure of it, too," Betty said. "I think they'd like the idea of Moose Hill continuing as it is."

"As it is, only better," Barry corrected her. Then he sighed again. "But what's the point of thinking about that now? Fred called just this morning to say the deal should be worked out around the time camp ends next week."

Stevie hardly heard him. She was still turning the number he had mentioned over in her mind, and it was making her head spin. Thirty thousand dollars! That was real money, and she knew it. Despite her natural optimism, she was having a hard time believing that even The Saddle Club could find a way to solve this problem.

But as she and Carole got up and said good-bye to Barry and Betty, one thought emerged clearly from Stevie's muddled brain. It might seem impossible, but they had to save Moose Hill. They just had to!

By the next day, Stevie hadn't come up with any ideas, though she had thought about it until her brain hurt. The girls talked about the problem while they cooled down their horses after one of their morning classes. "Our only chance is to raise enough money for Barry to buy the camp instead of the developers," Carole said for about the tenth time that day.

"Definitely," Stevie answered for the tenth time. Belle nudged her on the shoulder, and Stevie rubbed the mare's nose thoughtfully. "But how?"

As usual, none of them had an answer.

After a few minutes of silence, Stevie let out a long sigh. "There's got to be a way," she said. "There's *got* to!"

"Where there's a will there's a way," Carole said. It was

one of her father's favorite sayings. "We've got the will, right? So where's the way?"

"I hate to say it, but I'm not sure there *is* a way for a bunch of kids to raise thirty thousand dollars in a few days," Lisa said, switching Major's lead line from her right hand to her left as the horse wandered over to snuffle at Starlight. "That's more money than a lot of people earn in a whole year at their jobs."

"We can't just give up," Stevie said, a little annoyed at Lisa's tone. She knew thirty thousand dollars was a lot of money—they all did. Lisa didn't have to lecture them about it. "Carole's right. Where there's a will, there's a way."

Lisa just shrugged, and Stevie bit back the urge to snap at her for being negative. This was no time to start fighting with her friends, even if one friend wasn't being much of a team player at the moment.

Carole sensed the tension between Stevie and Lisa, and she didn't like it. "Maybe we should go over the ideas we've had so far," she suggested. "I know none of them seem that great, but maybe they'll inspire something."

"So far our best plan is Todd's idea to hold a giant skateboarding rally," Stevie admitted sadly. "The others, like getting a list of the richest people in the world and calling them to ask for a donation, don't seem too likely to work."

Carole sighed. It seemed hopeless, and for a second she

felt like giving up. But when she thought of the wonderful camp and all its beautiful forested land about to be gobbled up by greedy bulldozers, she knew they couldn't give up until they'd done everything they could. They wouldn't be The Saddle Club otherwise. "All right, we'll keep thinking," she said. "Let's just hope someone comes up with something brilliant pretty soon."

"I wish Piper were here to help us," Lisa said softly. "She's so smart—she could come up with a good plan if anyone could." The night before, she had taken a few minutes out of her reading time and written Piper a letter. Since she wasn't having any luck reaching her by phone, she decided it was time to try some other way. She had mailed it that morning from the rec hall.

Carole glanced at her watch. "Sorry to change the subject," she said, "but we'd better get back in the ring, Lisa. Our jump class starts in five minutes."

"Uh-oh," Stevie said, glancing automatically at her own wrist before realizing she had left her watch in the cabin again. "That means I have only five minutes to untack Belle and get over to the rec hall for my horsemanship class." She hurried toward the stable, barely pausing to say good-bye to her friends.

As she quickly untacked Belle, Stevie's thoughts returned to their problem. Every time she thought of a plan, she was brought up short by the huge amount of money they needed. She had to figure out a way to cut the problem down to size. Maybe then she'd be able to solve it.

Todd was in the same jump class as Carole and Lisa, and he rode forward to greet them as they entered the ring.

"Had any brilliant ideas yet?" he asked.

Carole shook her head. "I was about to ask you the same question."

Todd grinned. "Not yet," he replied. "But it's only a matter of time." He tapped his forehead meaningfully. "In some states this is registered as a lethal weapon, you know."

Carole laughed and glanced at Lisa. But Lisa didn't seem to be paying attention. As Betty entered the ring and called the class to order, Carole couldn't help wondering what was going on with Lisa these days. Judging from her behavior, it seemed she wasn't that upset about the camp's being sold. But Carole knew that Lisa loved Moose Hill as much as anybody else. That meant that something else must be bothering her an awful lot to distract her this much. So why hadn't she told her best friends about it?

"Okay, everyone," called Betty after a few opening comments. "We're going to take turns over the course and criticize each other's performance. Don't forget about your jump position, people—it might not matter if you're entering the show-jumping event, but you've got to have it down if you want to win points in the hunter classes." She nodded to Todd, who was riding a camp horse named Alamo. "You're first."

As she watched Todd start through the course, Carole remembered Lisa's comment about Piper. She hadn't really thought about it much, but she supposed Lisa must miss Piper a lot. And it couldn't be easy not knowing what had happened to her.

When Todd and Alamo had finished, they stopped in front of Betty. "Well?" Todd said with a grin. "Was I perfect or what?"

The other campers giggled. Alamo had knocked down two rails, and Todd had made several other obvious mistakes during the round.

"I'm not sure you're ready for the National Horse Show just yet," Betty replied dryly.

"Darn!" Todd cried. "I guess I'll have to withdraw my name. And I bet they won't refund my entry fee, either!"

The other campers laughed out loud at that, and even Betty had to smile. "Very funny," she said. She turned to the other riders. "Now, who would like to tell our class clown how he could have improved that ride?"

Carole's thoughts drifted again as several people gave their comments. She wondered if she and Stevie had underestimated the impact that Piper's disappearance was having on Lisa. Stevie was too focused on saving Moose Hill to think about much else, but maybe Carole should try to get to the bottom of the mystery and put Lisa's mind at ease. She would make tracking down Piper her own personal Saddle Club project.

"Okay, that's enough," Betty said after a few minutes of discussion about Todd's ride. "Thank you, Todd."

"Anytime," Todd said, doing his best to bow while still on horseback. "I'm thrilled that my mistakes could be of service."

"Glad to know we can count on you." Betty turned to survey the group. "Who wants to go next? Lisa, how about you?"

Carole watched as her friend rode forward to begin the course. Most of the riders were still smiling at Todd's clowning, but Lisa's face was serious. In fact, it was so serious that Carole couldn't help thinking that she might want to do more than look for answers about Piper. She might want to start keeping a closer eye on Lisa, too, at least until she could reassure herself that nothing was wrong with her.

Lisa's ride was much better than Todd's, but she didn't look very happy as she finished the course. In fact, she looked as pale and grim as Carole had ever seen her. As she watched her friend's set, determined expression, Carole didn't think she was going to be reassured anytime soon.

"WHERE IS SHE?" Phil asked later that evening. "I can't believe she's keeping us in suspense like this."

Carole shrugged. She, Phil, Todd, and Lisa were perched on the fence of the corral waiting for Stevie to show up. "All I know is she claims to have come up with the perfect plan to save this place," she said. She found it hard to believe, but as she watched several horses grazing in the evening coolness, she crossed her fingers hopefully.

Lisa glanced at her watch. She was eager to get back to her books—she was almost halfway through *Brave New World*—but she had to admit she was curious about Stevie's plan. Stevie had been bursting with it since arriving in the mess hall for dinner, but several other campers had sat down at their table before she could share it. As soon as the meal ended, she had asked them to wait for her at the corral, then disappeared.

She didn't keep them waiting for long. She arrived a moment later at a run, clutching a small notebook and a bright purple colored pencil.

"Good, you're all here," she said breathlessly.

"Nice pencil," Todd commented.

"I borrowed it from the arts and crafts room," Stevie explained. "I wanted to make some notes, because I've really got it this time. We're going to turn the horse show into a real fund-raising event!"

Carole collapsed against the fence, disappointed. "Is that it?" she said. "We thought of that already, remember? We figured out there's no way to make enough money, even if we charge a high ticket price and sell lemonade for five dollars a cup. There just won't be enough people at the show."

"Wait," Stevie said, holding up her hand. "You didn't let me explain. We're not just going to sell tickets and charge for refreshments—though of course we'll do that, too. Every little bit helps."

"What then?" Todd asked. "Come on, the suspense is killing us."

Stevie smiled. "We're going to ask people to sponsor the riders."

Carole, Phil, and Todd looked confused, but Lisa raised an eyebrow, looking interested. "Sponsor them?" she asked. "You mean like in a charity run?"

"Exactly," Stevie said. "Except instead of pledging a certain amount per mile, like in a run, our sponsors will pledge to donate a certain amount for each fence their rider jumps cleanly."

Lisa nodded slowly. Her mother volunteered for several charities, so Lisa knew a little about fund-raising. In this method, each competitor was responsible for signing up sponsors ahead of time, then collecting the money from them after the event. "It's an interesting idea, and I'm sure we could raise quite a bit of money that way. But thirty thousand dollars?"

Stevie flipped open the notebook and showed her friends a page of hastily scribbled numbers. "I've got it all figured out," she said. "There are about fifty riders at camp, right? And each of them will probably attempt at least eighteen fences during the show."

"Six in hunter seat equitation, and twelve in either hunter or show jumping," Carole said, nodding. She wasn't sure she completely understood this plan yet, but she couldn't help feeling hopeful. She kept her fingers crossed and did her best to cross her toes, too.

"The way I figure it," Stevie said, pointing at a row of figures on the notebook page, "each camper only has to get twelve people to sponsor them for three dollars per fence, and we'll be home free with money to spare."

Phil took the notebook and checked the numbers for himself. "That's right," he said. "It comes to $32,400." He shook his head in amazement. "You know, it's hard to believe this is the result of your lifetime C-plus average in math. You should turn in this notebook as an extracredit project next year."

Stevie just grinned. She could tell Phil was impressed, and that was nice. But the more important thing was that her plan would work. She was sure of it.

"There's just one problem," Carole pointed out. "Not everyone is going to clear every fence." She glanced at Lisa for support.

Lisa misinterpreted the glance, thinking that Carole meant that Lisa would be one of the riders who failed to ride clean. "You never know," she said quickly, her face once again taking on a grim, determined expression. "Some riders might do just that."

Carole was surprised by Lisa's reaction, and it worried her more than ever. So far she hadn't had any success in finding out what had happened to Piper—Barry wouldn't tell her a thing—but she was determined to keep trying.

Stevie didn't seem to notice Lisa's comment. "I thought about that, and I don't think we have to worry about a few downed rails here and there," she said. "There's sure to be a jump-off for the show-jumping event, and that means more fences for the people who make it. Besides, I'm hoping most people will get more than twelve sponsors. I'm sure it will all balance out in the end."

"Maybe," Phil said, sounding a little dubious. "But do you think all the sponsors are going to want to shell out three bucks a fence?"

"Good point. For eighteen fences . . ." Lisa quickly did the math in her head. "That's fifty-four dollars total. That's a lot of money, especially when we have such a short time to convince people to sponsor us."

"Never mind that," Carole said. "I just thought of another problem. Barry wanted us to keep the camp's sale a secret, remember? He's never going to let us do this."

But Stevie had already thought of that, too. "There's only one person who's going to have a secret kept from him, and that's Barry," she said. "Well, better make that Barry and the rest of the staff. We'll just spread the news quietly among the kids. I'm sure everyone will want to help out when they hear. Once the show is over and the money is ours, we'll break the good news to Barry. There's no way he can be mad at us then, right?"

"Right," Todd said. A smile spread across his face. "You know, Stevie, Phil keeps telling me what a dullard you are, but I think he's wrong about that. You're a genius!"

"I know," Stevie replied modestly. She turned to Carole and Lisa with a grin. "Well? What do you think?"

"I guess it's worth a try," Lisa said. "It's certainly the best plan we've come up with so far."

It wasn't exactly a rousing statement of support, but Stevie decided it would do. "Carole?"

Carole took a deep breath. "Let's do it," she said with a grin. "There's just one more thing I think we need. I think we have to confide in at least one adult about this—you know, to help us with the financial stuff."

Phil nodded. "I think that's a good idea," he said. "We'll need someone to help us hammer out the details."

Stevie thought she had hammered out most of the details pretty well already, but she decided the point wasn't worth arguing about. "Okay, if you insist," she said. "But who? It has to be someone we can trust."

"How about Betty?" Todd suggested.

"No way," Stevie said. "She and Barry are like this." She crossed her fingers. "She'd definitely rat on us."

Carole thought about the rest of the staff. "I've got it," she said after a moment. "Mike!"

"You mean Mike the stable hand?" Lisa asked. Mike was a laid-back, cheerful young man who had been working at Moose Hill for several summers. He was a favorite with all the campers, including The Saddle Club.

Phil nodded. "He's cool. I'm sure he'd help us out."

"Well . . ." Stevie still didn't like the idea of bringing an adult into their plan. But Mike *was* awfully great. In fact, most of the time he hardly seemed like an adult at all. "I guess that would be okay."

The five friends hurried into the stable. They found Mike in the tack room cleaning a bridle. "Yo," he greeted them with a smile.

The others glanced at Stevie, waiting for her to start. "Mike, we've got a favor to ask you . . . ," she began, then proceeded to tell him the whole story.

When she got to the part about the developers, Mike nodded. "Can't say I'm totally surprised," he admitted. "I've seen the suits hanging around, and, let's face it, Barry's mood has been a real roller coaster lately. I was starting to put two and two together." He sighed. "It's a real shame. This is a great place, and it's been a lot of fun for me. I'll hate to see it end."

"That's kind of what we wanted to talk to you about," Stevie said. "We want to make sure it *doesn't* end." She told him about her plan, speaking so quickly that her words started to get jumbled together.

Mike seemed to understand every word anyway. By the end of Stevie's speech, he was nodding. "Awesome plan, Stevie!" he exclaimed. "I never would have thought of it. I'm not sure you'll really be able to pull it off—I mean, the thirty thousand bucks. But if you want my help, I'm definitely your man. It's worth a try, right? And by the way, you can put me down right now for a three-thousand-dollar loan if Barry wants it." He shrugged. "I wish it could be more, but that's all I've got in my savings account."

"Great," Stevie said. To her friends' astonishment, she pulled a small calculator out of her shorts pocket and punched in some numbers. "That means each rider needs only *ten* sponsors at three dollars a fence."

"Where did you get that?" Carole asked.

Stevie held up the calculator so that Carole could see the number at the top. "It's right here on the calculator, see?"

"I know," Carole said. "I meant, where did you get the calculator?"

Stevie grinned. "I'll never tell." She winked at Phil. "You didn't *really* think I figured out all those numbers in my straight-C-plus head, did you?"

THE NEXT MORNING, Stevie spent every spare moment on one of the pay phones in the rec hall, calling everyone she knew who might sponsor her. She also did her best to spread the word about the fund-raiser to as many campers as possible. Most of them were horrified at the thought of Moose Hill closing and promised to do what they could to help. But to Stevie's annoyance, some people seemed downright disinterested in the whole thing.

"Can you believe it?" she fumed to Carole when she ran into her in the tack room between classes. "I just talked to that girl Arianna from Cabin Two, and she said she couldn't care less whether Moose Hill gets bulldozed."

Carole shook her head as she hung Starlight's bridle on a hook on the wall. She had received one or two similar responses herself. "Luckily, she's in the minority," she said. "Most of the people I told are dying to help."

"Good." Stevie grabbed the saddle soap and started to clean Belle's saddle as quickly as possible. "How many sponsors do you have so far?"

"Not many," Carole said. She leaned against the wall and started ticking off the list on her fingers. "Just my dad—he said he wants to sponsor you and Lisa, too, by the way—and his secretary, and my relatives in Florida. Oh, and I called Pine Hollow, and Red said he'd sponsor The Saddle Club as a group."

"Great," Stevie said. Red O'Malley was the head stable hand at Pine Hollow. "But you've got to get more sponsors."

"I will," Carole promised. "My dad is going to call my relatives in Minnesota, and he'll also talk to some of our neighbors and his friends at work. And I've got a list of friends from school that I have to call."

Stevie nodded. "I already talked to Max, and he and Deborah are sponsoring all three of us for five dollars a fence." Deborah was Max's wife.

"Fantastic," Carole said. "If everyone is that generous, we'll have more than enough money before all this is over."

"Keep your fingers crossed," Stevie said. She gave the saddle one last swipe with her rag and stood up. "I've got to run. I have a free period next, and I want to make some more calls."

Carole nodded. "Lisa has a free period now, too," she reminded her. "Maybe you two can coordinate your efforts. As for me, I've got an unmounted class. So I guess I'll see you at lunch."

The two parted ways, and Stevie hurried out of the stable, patting her pocket to make sure the calling card her parents had given her was still there. But she stopped short at the sight that greeted her just outside. Lisa was riding Major toward the jump course that was set up at one end of the meadow.

"What are you doing?" Stevie cried, running toward her. "I thought you had a free period now."

"I do." Lisa glanced down at her friend from Major's back. "I'm going to go through the course a few times and then practice lead changes for a while."

Stevie could hardly believe her ears. "But you have calls to make!" she exclaimed. "Sponsors to seek! Money to raise! Don't tell me you've forgotten already."

"Of course not," Lisa said, sounding a little annoyed. "But I have a lot of other things to do, too. I'll make my calls later."

"When?" Stevie said. "We don't exactly have months to spare, you know."

Lisa sighed. "Look, I'll spend part of the lunch hour on the phone, okay? I promise."

Stevie decided she would have to be satisfied with that. She left Lisa to her riding and raced to the rec hall.

Her first call was to her house. She had spoken to her

parents earlier that morning, but none of her three brothers had been home at the time.

Her twin, Alex, picked up the phone. "Oh, it's you," he said, sounding less than thrilled.

"Nice to hear your voice, too," Stevie said sarcastically. Then she remembered why she was calling and decided to try to be nice. "Um, so how's it going?"

She could almost hear her brother shrug over the phone. "It's going," Alex said. "Mom and Dad are both out. So if you're calling to ask for money, you'll have to try again later." He laughed loudly at his own joke.

Stevie gritted her teeth and did her best to keep her voice pleasant. "Actually, it's funny you should mention money," she said. "I have sort of a favor to ask." She quickly filled him in on the situation. "So how about it?" she finished. "How much should I put you down for? Does three dollars a fence sound about right?"

Alex snorted. "Try *negative* three dollars," he said. "That way you'll owe *me* money—if that mangy horse of yours makes it over any fences, that is."

Stevie clutched the phone cord so hard that her fingernails dug into her palm. She hoped all her sponsors weren't going to be this annoying. "Come on, Alex," she said, her voice getting dangerously close to a whine. "I'm serious about this. If I don't get enough sponsors, Moose Hill will close." Suddenly she remembered something. "Besides, I'd hate to have to be the one to tell Mom and

72

Dad that you snuck out after curfew to meet your girl-friend that time."

"Hmm." Alex paused to think about that for a moment. "Well, I guess that stupid camp serves some purpose—it keeps you away from here for a few weeks every summer."

"Right," Stevie said brightly. "So how much is that worth to you? Two bucks a fence? Even a dollar would help."

"I'll give you ten cents a fence," Alex said.

"What!" Stevie exclaimed. "That's it? One lousy dime? Remember, you were out *way* after curfew—and it was a school night, too . . ."

"All right, a quarter a fence," Alex said. "But that's my final offer."

Stevie could tell he meant it. "Fine," she said. "I'll take what I can get. A quarter it is. Put Chad on, will you?"

As Alex yelled for their older brother, Stevie sank down to the floor and leaned against the wall. This wasn't going to be easy.

STEVIE DIDN'T SLOW down her efforts for the next couple of hours. She made more calls, she told more campers about the fund-raiser, and she urged the ones who already knew about it to keep on working at getting sponsors. In fact, she was so busy that she was almost late for her afternoon jump class. Although the girls had had separate classes that morning, The Saddle Club were all in this class together, along with Phil and Todd.

"Hi," she whispered to her friends, riding into the ring just as Betty called the class to order.

"We thought you weren't going to make it," Carole whispered back.

Stevie reached down to finish tightening Belle's girth. "Me too," she replied. "But I have some good news. My mom's law partner agreed to sponsor me. She's only pledging a dollar a fence, but that's more than some people are willing to give."

Phil glanced cautiously at Betty, who had turned to help another camper with her stirrups. "I know," he said. "You'd be surprised how many of the people I've asked think even a dollar is too much. My sister Barbara would only pledge a quarter a fence."

"She and Alex should get together," Stevie said. "Anyway, we're just going to have to make it up in volume. And Mike had a great idea about that. He offered to take a few of us into town tomorrow afternoon to look for sponsors." The next day was Saturday, and there were no afternoon classes. During time off, campers were sometimes allowed to make trips into the closest town, as long as Barry gave them permission.

"What are you going to tell Barry?" Lisa asked.

"I'll think of something," Stevie said. "I've got to. We need this trip if we're going to have any prayer of getting the kinds of numbers we need."

Just then Betty turned to glare at them. "Excuse me. Am I interrupting your discussion, kids?"

"Sorry," Carole said contritely.

"Okay then." Betty turned back to the rest of the class and continued. "As I was saying, it's almost time to decide whether you feel up to the challenges of show jumping or if you'd rather stick with hunter jumping."

Stevie sat up a little straighter. With all the excitement over her plan, she had almost forgotten about the show-jumping event.

"I want you to take this decision seriously," Betty went on. "You've got to be realistic about whether you're ready. Show jumping is a strenuous event for you and the horse. As you know, the pace is fast and the fences are higher than in hunter jumping—though of course ours won't be nearly as high as some of those you may have seen on TV."

"Whew," Todd said loudly, and the others laughed.

Betty smiled. "Okay, let's ride—once through the course, one at a time, at a canter. I know you're all probably dying to talk about the show, so go ahead. Just listen for me to call your name. Melissa, you're up first today."

As Melissa moved forward, Stevie turned to her friends again. "Well, we're almost to the moment of truth," she said with a grin. "Who's up for the challenge of show jumping? Besides me, that is."

"Count me in," Carole said eagerly. "I can't wait. It'll be a fantastic learning experience for Starlight."

"Oh, yeah, that's why I'm doing it, too," Phil said, turning to wink at Todd. He grinned. "Actually, I think it will be a blast. I'm in for sure."

Todd was shaking his head. "Sounds a little rich for my blood," he said. "I haven't been riding as long as the rest of you, and I happen to like my bones just the way they are—unbroken."

Stevie opened her mouth to tease Todd about his decision, but Carole shut her up with a sharp look. "I think that's a smart decision, Todd," she said. "When it comes to riding, better safe than sorry is a good rule. It never pays to rush things." She turned to Lisa. "Have you made a decision yet?"

"I made my decision ages ago," Lisa said without hesitation. "I'm going for it."

Carole and Stevie were surprised at her confident tone. Lisa was definitely a better rider than Todd, but she hadn't been riding a whole lot longer than he had. It was easy for her friends to forget that sometimes, but not now.

"Oh, right," Carole said uncertainly. "Um, I mean, that's good." She was afraid to say anything more—Lisa had been so touchy lately.

Stevie was entertaining similar thoughts. There was no way she was going to suggest that Lisa reconsider her decision, at least not directly. But when Phil and Todd rode off to talk to one of their cabin mates, she leaned closer to Lisa and winked at her.

"Are you really sure about this show jumping thing?"

she asked teasingly. "I mean, yeah, it's going to be exciting. But wouldn't it be even more exciting to be in the same class with hunky Todd?"

That was the last straw. "Okay, Stevie, I've had enough," Lisa exploded. "You've been hinting around about Todd all week, and I've told you over and over that I'm not interested in him. So cut it out, okay?" Major shifted uneasily under her, and she realized she was gripping the reins so hard that she was accidentally yanking on the bit. She loosened her grip, sending the horse a silent apology.

Stevie was taken aback. Lisa was usually so even-tempered and reasonable that her friends sometimes forgot she had a temper. "Sorry," Stevie said, wide-eyed. "I was just kidding around."

Lisa sighed. "I know," she said. "I'm sorry. I shouldn't be yelling about it. But I really wish you'd let up a little. Todd is a nice guy and everything, but I'm just not interested in finding a boyfriend at the moment. I have too many other things on my mind right now."

Just then Betty called Lisa's name, and she rode forward to begin the course. Stevie and Carole exchanged surprised glances. "What was that all about?" Carole asked. But at that moment Todd and Phil returned, and Stevie quickly changed the subject.

AFTER THE JUMP class, Lisa headed to the rec hall for an unmounted lecture while Stevie and Carole cooled their horses down in preparation for an equitation class. Phil and Todd were in a different class, so the girls finally had a chance to talk about Lisa.

"I can't believe the way she jumped down my throat," Stevie said. "I mean, she apologized right away, but still . . ."

Carole nodded. "I know. It's not like her." She glanced at Stevie. "You have to admit, though, you've been pretty relentless about this whole Todd-Lisa topic."

"Well, maybe," Stevie admitted, pausing to let Belle take a few sips of water from the trough by the stable entrance. "But I only had Lisa's best interests in mind. I thought maybe if she got interested in Todd, she'd forget about all the problems she had during the first two weeks here."

"You mean like Piper disappearing?" Carole said. "I know what you mean. I'm afraid Lisa is a lot more upset about that than she's letting on."

Stevie nodded. "I thought a nice summer romance would be the perfect solution."

"It was a good plan, even if it didn't exactly work," Carole said. "But I have a little plan of my own." She told Stevie about her attempts to find out what had happened to Piper. "Barry won't tell me a thing, and nobody else seems to know. I found Piper's home phone number on Lisa's bed—I think she's still trying to reach her, even though she hasn't mentioned it lately—but nobody answered when I called." She sighed. "It's as if she just disappeared into thin air."

Just then the instructor called to them. Class was starting. "We'll have to talk more about this later," Stevie said as they mounted and headed for the ring.

ABOUT HALFWAY THROUGH the equitation class, Barry stopped by to observe. Stevie and Belle were near the fence, waiting their turn to perform, when he arrived.

"Hi, Barry," Stevie said brightly. "You're just the person I wanted to see."

"Oh, really?" he said, looking slightly suspicious. "Why's that?"

"I need a pass to go into town tomorrow," Stevie replied. "Actually, a few of us were hoping to go."

Barry raised one eyebrow quizzically. "How many is a few? And why were you hoping to go?"

Stevie bent over to brush an imaginary fly from Belle's neck, stalling for time as she tried to think of a good answer. "Oh, six or eight of us, I guess," she said, trying to estimate how many people could fit into Mike's station wagon. "It's sort of—um—a reading group."

"A reading group?" Barry repeated, looking surprised.

Stevie nodded vigorously. "That's right," she said. "We want to go to the library and do some research on, uh, show jumping. You know, prepare for the show and everything. Mike already said he'd drive us. Can we go?"

Barry shrugged. "I don't see why not," he said. "Far be it from me to discourage young people from reading."

He still looked a little puzzled as he walked away, but Stevie just grinned. He would understand everything soon enough.

THE CLASS ENDED a few minutes early. Carole and Stevie headed to the rec hall to meet Lisa so that they could all walk back to the cabin together to change for dinner. They peeked into the room where Lisa's class was being held, but she was nowhere to be seen. Carole frowned. "Where is she?" she whispered.

Stevie shrugged. "Maybe she's sitting in the back."

But when the class let out, the girls couldn't find Lisa anywhere in the room. They stopped Helen, a girl from their cabin, to ask about her.

"She said she had a stomachache," Helen said. "It sounded like it might have been something she ate at lunch. She went back to the cabin to lie down."

Stevie and Carole exchanged concerned glances, then hurried out of the building. "Do you think Lisa's getting sick?" Carole asked. "Maybe that's why she's been acting so weird lately."

"Maybe." Stevie started walking a little faster, then broke into a jog.

Lisa looked up when her friends burst into the cabin. She was sitting on her bunk with a book in her hands.

"Hi," she said, looking and sounding perfectly healthy. "What's the matter?"

"That's what we want to know," Carole said breathlessly. "We heard you were sick."

Lisa shrugged. "I'm fine. I just said that to get out of class." She held up her book. "I started *Frankenstein* this morning, and I want to get through it quickly."

Carole frowned. It wasn't like Lisa to skip a class. It wasn't like her at all. "Are you sure you're all right?" she asked. "Um, you haven't exactly been yourself lately."

Stevie nodded. "Is there anything you want to talk about?" she asked. "I mean, we're your best friends. If you're having problems or something . . ."

"What's that supposed to mean?" Lisa snapped. "Just because I'm trying to be responsible and work on my reading list, you automatically assume I have a problem?"

"Well, no," Carole began hesitantly. "But—"

Lisa didn't give her a chance to go on. "Look, I'm fine, okay?" she said. "I know you guys don't understand why this stuff is so important to me, but it is. So believe me, I'm fine. Just back off, okay?"

"Okay," Stevie said quickly. She couldn't believe how easy it was to make Lisa angry these days. Maybe it was because she was staying up reading—Stevie had seen the flashlight glowing under the covers late into the night. "Um, it's almost dinnertime. Are you ready to go?"

Lisa looked down at her book, not meeting her friends'

eyes. "You guys go ahead," she said, her voice sounding calmer but still a little strained. "I want to finish this chapter. I'll meet you at the mess hall in a little while."

"Okay," Stevie and Carole said in one voice. They quickly changed out of their riding clothes and left the cabin without another word.

They saved a seat for Lisa all through dinner, but she never showed up.

THE NEXT DAY after lunch, Stevie, Carole, Lisa, Phil, Todd, and a few other campers piled into Mike's ancient, battered green station wagon for the trip into town.

"Next stop, Main Street," Mike sang out as he skillfully negotiated the old car down the rutted road leading to the highway.

Stevie was crushed into the front seat between Mike and Phil. "Anybody for a singalong?" she cried. Without waiting for an answer, she launched into an enthusiastic, if slightly off-key, rendition of "Ninety-nine Bottles of Beer on the Wall." She was in a good mood. After dinner the night before, Lisa had apologized for being so touchy and then had agreed to come along to the rec hall to make phone calls. Working together, Stevie, Carole, and Lisa had signed up another fifteen sponsors. And Stevie was feeling optimistic about their mission in town today. Their plan was going to work—it *had* to work.

The kids were down to forty-three bottles of beer on the wall when Mike pulled onto the main street of the small town. He drove past the small, grassy town square and found a parking place in front of the library. Stevie grinned, remembering the excuse she had given Barry.

"Okay, everybody out," Mike said, turning off the engine. "We've only got about three hours before we have to head back, so do your thing."

"Ugh," Carole grunted, trying to move enough to open the door. The backseat was so crowded that her arm was wedged against the armrest. Finally she managed to extricate herself. She waited on the sidewalk, rubbing her arm, while the others clambered out one by one. "I think I'll walk back to camp."

Stevie was already giving orders to her troops. "Carole and Lisa, why don't you two stake out the town square over there and talk to everyone who walks by," she said, pointing. "Todd and Melissa, you take the businesses right around here. Phil and I will head down that way and start knocking on some doors. Helen and Bev, you go the other way."

Carole gave her friend a crisp salute. "Aye, aye, captain," she said. "Let's go raise some money!"

The other kids let out a whoop, then parted ways. Mike

crossed the street to run some errands at the drugstore while Stevie and Phil hurried down a residential street.

"We can talk to more people if we split up," Phil pointed out. "I'll take this side of the street if you'll do the other side."

"Sounds good," Stevie said, smiling at him. It was no accident that she had paired herself with Phil. This stay at camp hadn't exactly been the romantic idyll she had pictured, but she would take romance where she could get it. Working together to save Moose Hill seemed pretty romantic to her. "We'll meet at the end of each block and compare notes."

Phil nodded, and Stevie crossed the street and approached a white clapboard house with a neat, flower-filled yard. At her knock, the door was opened by a petite, red-haired young woman holding a baby.

"Hi there," Stevie said. "My name is Stevie Lake, and I'm staying at Moose Hill Riding Camp, just down the road. A group of us are trying to save the camp from being sold to land developers, and I was wondering if you'd be willing to sponsor me in our horse show next week." She had rehearsed the speech all morning and had taught it to the others at lunch.

The woman smiled. "You're a Moose Hill camper?" she said. "That's wonderful. I spent some great summers there during high school." She sighed. "I couldn't believe it when I heard it was being sold. It's terrible."

"You mean you know about that already?" Stevie asked, surprised. From everything Barry had said, she had supposed the deal was a deep, dark secret known only to a few people.

The woman nodded. "Oh, yes," she said, jiggling the sleepy-looking baby up and down on her hip as she talked. "The sale has caused a lot of commotion around town. My husband is on the zoning commission, and they did their best to block the whole deal." She shook her head. "But it didn't work."

Stevie was fascinated. "Did your husband try to prevent the sale because you used to go there?"

The woman laughed. "Oh, no," she said. "Although that would be reason enough." She blushed. "It's where he and I first met."

Stevie's eyes widened. It seemed she and Phil weren't the first couple to be brought together by Moose Hill's magic! "Then why?" she asked.

"Everyone around here knows Moose Hill, and it's been a good neighbor over the years," the woman said. "Nobody wants to see it razed for a bunch of fancy vacation condos for rich people. This area has always been rural, and we like it that way. That's why most of us chose to live here."

Stevie smiled. If most of the townspeople were against the deal with the developers, their job would be even easier than she had hoped. "In that case," she said. "Would you be willing to help us out? We're asking people to sponsor us for a certain amount for each fence we clear during the show. The money we raise will help the camp director outbid the developers and buy the camp."

"What a great idea!" The woman laughed, startling the baby, who stared at Stevie with wide blue eyes. "How many fences are there?"

"Eighteen total," Stevie said, "plus six more if there's a jump-off in the show-jumping event."

"You're doing show jumping?" The woman looked impressed. "We never did that in my day."

Stevie nodded. "It's a new event," she said. "If you're interested in coming to watch, the show is next Friday." She gave the woman information about the schedule and ticket prices.

"I'll be there," the woman promised. "And you can put me and my husband down for two dollars a fence."

Stevie took down the woman's name, address, and phone number, then said good-bye and moved on to the next house. She couldn't help whistling a little as she walked. Things were definitely looking up for Moose Hill.

NOT EVERYBODY WAS as eager to help as the red-haired woman, but Carole and Lisa were also finding that most of the people they spoke to were on their side. Almost everyone they asked agreed to pledge at least a little bit of money, and soon they had signed up more than ten sponsors.

During the lulls when nobody was walking by, Carole

kept herself busy by thinking about Lisa. She was acting more like her normal self today, but Carole wasn't convinced it was going to last.

She decided she had to try to talk to Lisa again, even if it meant making her angry. "Lisa," she began tentatively when no townspeople were in sight. "I kind of wanted to talk to you about yesterday."

"I understand," Lisa said immediately. "I was really rotten to you guys, and I'm sorry about that." She shrugged and smiled, brushing a strand of hair out of her eyes. "I guess I stayed up too late reading the night before or something."

"That's not exactly what I meant," Carole replied. She didn't think Lisa's moodiness resulted only from sleep deprivation. There was just too much odd behavior to excuse that way. "You already apologized for that yesterday. But I'm still kind of surprised you decided to skip class."

"I know," Lisa said. "But it was a one-time thing, really. I knew we were going to be talking about bandaging, and since Max has drilled everything there is to know about the topic into us over and over again, I thought I'd give myself a break and do some reading."

"Oh." Carole thought about that for a second. It sounded reasonable, but she wasn't completely reassured. "Well, what about missing dinner like you did last night? It wasn't the first time you skipped a meal in the past couple of weeks."

"I guess that's true," Lisa said, leaning against a tree next to the sidewalk. She shrugged again. "It's just that I get so hungry after all that riding. Sometimes I can't wait for mealtime." She laughed. "Believe me, whoever gets the money from those snack machines in the rec hall must love me. And once I've pigged out on that stuff, the last thing I want to do is go to the mess hall and look at more food."

"All that junk food can't be good for you," Carole said, concerned.

"It's not all bad," Lisa said, straightening up as an elderly couple approached. "Besides, eating that stuff for a couple of weeks won't kill me."

The girls stepped forward to talk to the elderly couple. Once they had signed them up for fifty cents per fence, they relaxed again.

"I hope you don't think Stevie and I have been nagging you lately," Carole said. "I mean, about your reading and the extra riding practice and everything. We're just worried that you're pushing yourself too hard. Camp is supposed to be fun."

"You don't have to worry about me," Lisa said. "I like hard work. I'm having a great time at camp. Everything is fine."

Carole wasn't sure what to think. She wanted to believe what Lisa was saying. After all, the members of The Saddle Club didn't lie to each other. It wasn't exactly an official rule, but it was something Carole had always taken for granted. That was why she didn't like her present suspicion—because it was telling her that Lisa was lying.

Before she could explore that thought any further, a group of teenage girls wandered around the corner and headed for them.

"Hey, there they are!" cried one of the girls. She hurried toward Carole and Lisa. "We heard you're raising money to save the riding camp."

"That's right," Carole said and launched into her spiel, pushing her concern about Lisa to the back of her mind. It was too hard to think seriously about the problem and look for sponsors at the same time. Carole was almost glad there was only one more week of camp. Maybe once they were home, Lisa would go back to normal.

LATER THAT EVENING, back at camp, Stevie and Phil set off hand in hand for a romantic stroll down to the pond, just like the day they had met. Unlike that first night, this night a full moon illuminated the paths for them, casting a romantic silvery glow over everything and making flashlights unnecessary.

"This is nice," Phil said as they picked their way carefully over the narrow, rocky path.

Stevie didn't answer.

"Stevie?" Phil prompted. "Did you hear me? I said, this is nice."

"Oh, right," Stevie said. "Sorry. I was just thinking

about something else. I was wondering if I should have started off our speech today by suggesting that people donate three dollars a fence. I don't know about you, but most of the people I talked to didn't pledge anywhere near that much."

Phil shrugged. "Who knows? It's too late now." As they reached the edge of the pond, he dropped her hand and put his arm around her. "Aren't there other things you'd rather think about right now, anyway?" he added softly.

Stevie nodded and tipped her head up to gaze into his eyes. "I wonder if we could convince the cook to bake some cookies before the show?" she murmured. "We could sell them to the spectators. I have a feeling we're going to have a big crowd this year."

"Whatever," Phil said. "Did I ever tell you your hair looks really pretty in the moonlight?"

"No, I don't think so," she said distractedly. She pulled away from his embrace and fished in her pocket for her calculator. "Let's see, if we charged fifty cents per cookie . . . um . . ." She hunched over the calculator and punched in some numbers, squinting to see the readout in the dim light.

Phil sighed and sat down on a boulder. "Did I ever tell you about the time I was abducted by space aliens?" he said.

"Hmm? Oh, that's nice," Stevie muttered, still punching in numbers. Then she reached into her pocket again and pulled out a folded sheet of paper she had torn out of her notebook. She scanned it and then returned to her calculator. "I can't believe it," she cried a moment later. "Even with all the sponsors we've gotten so far, we're still way short of what we need. And that's assuming no one misses a single fence."

Phil got up and came over to her. "Do you have to do that now?" he asked. He caressed her cheek gently. "I was hoping we could just forget about it and have a nice, romantic evening."

"Well, maybe . . . ," she said, closing her eyes as Phil moved in for a kiss. But just as his lips grazed hers, her eyes flew open. "I'm sorry," she said, moving away from him and raising her calculator again. "I can't stop thinking about the fund-raiser. We just don't have enough money pledged yet. And if we don't do something about that in the next few days, we can forget about any more romantic evenings here at Moose Hill ever again!"

WITH EVERYTHING THE Saddle Club and their friends had to do, the following days passed in a blur. On Sunday, Stevie spent three hours on the phone, calling everyone she knew from school, Pine Hollow, and everywhere else she could think of. She called her friends at the County Animal Rescue League. She spoke to Chelsea Webber, Belle's previous owner. She contacted her friend Dinah in Vermont. She even tracked down Mrs. McCurdy, the old woman who had lived next door when Stevie was in kindergarten. Every one of them promised to contribute, though Mrs. McCurdy only pledged ten cents per jump.

Stevie was glad that Carole had offered to get in touch with The Saddle Club's friends at the Bar None Ranch out West, and that Lisa was in charge of trying to contact their friend Skye Ransom, a movie star who lived in California. Even so, she had the funniest feeling that her parents were going to be a little surprised at all the charges on her calling card. She would just have to deal with that later.

MONDAY MORNING WAS cloudy. Carole, Phil, and Todd had a free period at the same time, so they decided to go talk to the camp cook about Stevie's cookie idea. They found him chopping vegetables for dinner.

Carole did the talking, explaining that they were hoping he could manage to make two or three hundred cookies for the show on Friday.

The cook put down his knife. "Oh, really?" he said, looking amused. "Is that two or three hundred cookies in addition to the lemonade and iced tea and popcorn I'm already planning to provide?"

Carole and the boys nodded. "Actually, we should probably talk to you about that, too," Phil said. "We may have a few more spectators coming to the show this year than usual."

"Yeah, a few *hundred* more," Todd added with a grin.

"Really?" the cook said with a slight frown. "How do you know? Are you talking about parents? I thought we were filming the show again this year." Since most parents couldn't make it up to camp a day early to watch the show, Barry always had one of the stable hands videotape

94

the whole thing. That way, any interested parents—or any camper who wanted a memento—could borrow the tape and make a copy.

Carole's eyes lit up. "I wonder if Stevie remembers about the videos," she whispered to Phil. "We could sell those, too."

"Sell them?" the cook asked. Apparently his ears were as sharp as his knife. "What do you mean? What's this really all about?"

Phil tried to change the subject back to cookies, but the cook wouldn't leave them alone until they had told him the whole story. His eyes widened when he heard about the developers. "So that's who those guys were," he muttered. "I wondered why they kept hanging around Barry's office."

"You won't tell Barry what we're doing, will you?" Carole begged.

The cook grinned. "Nah," he said. "Old Barry is a great guy—I've known him so long he's like the brother I never had—but sometimes he's too stubborn for his own good. If he's convinced the camp is lost, he won't change his mind until someone forces him to. If you kids really think you can do it, more power to you."

"So how about those cookies?" Todd prompted hopefully.

"You can count on me," the cook replied. "You'll have your cookies, even if I have to stay up all night making them."

95

* * *

TUESDAY AT LUNCH, Lisa stared at her grilled cheese sandwich, willing herself not to eat it. Her stomach was growling hungrily—she had skipped breakfast to work with Major—and she loved grilled cheese. But she was determined to stick to her diet, and the sandwich was much too fattening to allow herself even one bite. Instead she speared a cucumber slice with her fork and popped it into her mouth, chewing slowly and carefully to make it last longer. After eating a little more salad and a few bites of cole slaw, she carefully cut the sandwich into three pieces. Then she waited until Carole and Stevie weren't looking and slipped one of the pieces into a napkin in her lap. She repeated the process twice more until the entire sandwich had disappeared from her plate. It was the easiest way to keep her friends from finding out about her diet and asking lots of pesky questions. What they didn't know wouldn't hurt them.

STEVIE WAS CLEANING Belle's bridle on Wednesday afternoon when Mike raced into the tack room, looking frantic. "Bad news," he said when he saw her. "Someone must have clued in the local TV station about our little project. There's a news team headed for Barry's office right now."

Stevie gasped and dropped the bridle. The bit landed on her foot, but she hardly noticed. "We've got to stop them!" she cried. "If Barry finds out now, it will ruin everything!" She raced outside with Mike right behind her.

The news truck was parked in the driveway near the mess hall, and several people were climbing out. One had a large video camera on his shoulder, and another had a microphone in her hand.

"Hi," Stevie gasped, skidding to a stop in front of them.

The woman with the microphone looked a little surprised. "Hi there, young lady," she said. "Who might you be?"

"Well, I might be the President of the United States someday," she said with a grin. "But for now I'm Stevie Lake, a camper here."

The reporter looked puzzled by Stevie's joke. "Um, in that case maybe you could point us toward the camp director's office," she said. "I'd like to interview him about the fund-raiser he's running here."

Stevie gulped and glanced at Mike. He looked just as panicked as she felt. Suddenly she remembered something Carole had mentioned the other day, and relief washed over her. "I've got it!" she exclaimed. "Oops, I mean, of course I'll point you toward the camp director." She winked at Mike and pointed to the mess hall. "He's in there. Mike will take you inside if you want—I've got to go." As she raced past a confused-looking Mike, she hissed, "Just play along!"

When Mike led the news team into the mess hall a

moment later, Stevie and the cook were there to meet them. Stevie hid the cook's apron behind her back and grinned as he stepped forward to meet the visitors.

"Hi there," the cook said, extending his hand. "I'm Barry, the camp director. How can I help you?"

"I STILL CAN'T believe you got those reporters to believe the cook was Barry," Carole told Stevie the next day at breakfast.

Stevie winked at her smugly. "Where there's a will, there's a way," she said. "I'm just glad you guys had filled him in on our whole plan so he knew what to say."

"*I'm* just glad Barry doesn't watch much TV," Phil put in, wiping orange juice off his chin. "Can you imagine if he'd turned on the news and saw the camp cook posing as him?"

Carole grinned at the thought. Then her grin faded as she glanced over at the empty seat beside her. She had been saving it for Lisa, but so far Lisa hadn't shown up. Carole quickly drained her milk glass and stood up. "I'm finished," she said. "I'll meet you guys at the stable, okay? I've got to check on something back in the cabin."

She found Lisa reading on her bunk.

"Hi," Lisa greeted her without looking up from her book.

"Hi," Carole replied. She cleared her throat. "Breakfast is almost over. I thought you were going to come join us once you finished your chapter."

This time Lisa glanced up briefly before returning her attention to the page in front of her. "Sorry about that," she mumbled. "I kind of got caught up in the story."

Carole waited for her to say something more, but it was as if Lisa had already forgotten she was there. "Aren't you hungry?" she said at last. It wasn't what she had wanted to ask, but she didn't know the right way to ask her if she was ever going to start acting normal again.

Lisa just shrugged. "Not really. I had a huge dinner last night."

Carole remembered that they had had cheeseburgers and home fries the evening before. Now that she thought about it, Lisa's plate had been clean when dinner was over. "Okay," she said uncertainly. "Well, classes start pretty soon. Do you want to walk up to the stable with me?"

"You go ahead," Lisa said, turning a page. "I'll catch up in a minute."

Lisa didn't look up from her book until she heard the cabin door close behind Carole. Then she let out a long, loud sigh. Carole was getting nosier and nosier. Lisa was starting to have trouble coming up with enough excuses to satisfy her.

She rubbed her stomach, thinking about the breakfast

she had just missed, imagining what it would have tasted like. But she quickly shoved those thoughts out of her mind and did her best to concentrate on her book. She was a little worried about her reading—she still had more than half a dozen books to read, and that meant she was going to have to find more time somewhere. Maybe she could stay up later and wake up earlier in the morning. It wasn't going to be easy, but nothing important ever was, was it?

Besides, it would all be worth it, she told herself. Soon she would be able to show her friends, her parents—the world—that she wasn't playing catch-up anymore. She would prove that she, like Piper, had her life together at last. When she finished the last book on her list and won the blue ribbon in show jumping, her life would finally be perfect.

BEFORE ANYONE QUITE realized it, it was the day of the show. It was a perfect summer day, with a flawlessly blue sky stretching from horizon to horizon. People started pouring down the hard-packed dirt road an hour before the first event was scheduled to start, and before long the seating area was filled to capacity.

Stevie came across Barry near the stable entrance. He was peering in confusion at the crowd milling around outside. "Where are they all coming from?" he muttered to himself.

Stevie stepped forward and tugged on his sleeve. "It seems to be getting kind of crowded out there," she said innocently. "Do you want me to round up some kids and bring out the chairs from the mess hall?"

"Good idea," Barry said. "Thanks, Stevie. You're a real help."

As she hurried away, Stevie grinned. "You don't know the half of it," she said under her breath.

It didn't take long for the new supply of chairs to be filled as well, but most of the spectators didn't seem to mind standing. They milled around the meadow, munching on the cook's delicious chocolate chip cookies (fifty cents apiece) and commenting on the lovely scenery and the gorgeous day. By showtime, the camp's parking area was overflowing, and still the people kept coming, parking along the road and walking the rest of the way.

"This is great," Carole said when she ran into Stevie coming out of the tack room. "Can you believe how many people came?"

"Of course I can believe it," Stevie said airily. "Who wouldn't want to come to our horse show?"

One of the instructors happened to be walking by at the moment, and she overheard Stevie's words. "Who, indeed?" she commented with a wink and a grin before hurrying on her way. By this time, most of the staff knew about the fund-raiser. Some had seen the news story and had asked the cook about it; others had overheard campers talking or had been told by friends in town. Barry and Betty were just about the only ones who were still in the dark about the whole thing.

Just then Phil walked past, leading his horse, Teddy. "Phil!" Stevie exclaimed. "Did you have a chance to talk to Barry about the videotapes?"

"Mission accomplished," Phil said. "I convinced him that all the parents would appreciate the tapes even more if they had to pay for them instead of getting them for free."

Stevie laughed. That sounded like something she might say. "And that worked?"

"Well, not really," Phil said with a shrug. "But then I suggested that he could use the money for staff bonuses— you know, when he tells them the camp is closing down. That did it."

They stopped talking as Betty hustled past, carrying a clipboard. "Better get a move on, people," she said when she spotted them. "The dressage event starts in fifteen minutes flat."

In between her fund-raising efforts and everything else, Stevie had somehow managed to find the energy to work hard with Belle in all their classes, especially dressage. The practice paid off, and at the end of the event, they rode away with the blue ribbon. Phil came in second, and Carole was third.

Lisa, who had come in seventh, watched as all kinds of people came up to congratulate Stevie on her win.

"Don't worry about it, boy," she whispered to Major, rubbing his nose as she walked him to cool him down. "This one didn't matter. We'll have our turn in the spotlight a little later."

After dressage came hunter seat equitation. This was an event in which the rider's ability was judged, rather than the horse's. First each competitor jumped a course of six low fences. Then the judges called the riders back into the ring one by one and asked them to perform various maneuvers and gaits.

Stevie held her breath during the jumping portion of the event, and it wasn't because she was worried about her own performance. Every time a hoof grazed a rail, she winced, and the few times a fence came down, she groaned out loud. She could almost hear the cash slipping away with each mistake. There were only about a dozen jumping faults in the entire group, but Stevie wasn't comforted. The equitation fences weren't supposed to be very challenging. The real test would come later, in the hunter-jumping and show-jumping events.

Stevie was so distracted that she ended up placing out of the ribbons in equitation, but she didn't really mind. She cheered loudly for Carole, who had come in first, and Phil, who was fourth.

As the hunter-jumping event got underway, Stevie pulled out her calculator and did her best to figure out how many rails the riders could afford to miss. But the fund-raising project had become so huge and complicated that she really wasn't certain how close they were to their goal. She could make a pretty good estimate about the take from the ticket and food sales, but beyond that it was anybody's guess how much money they had raised so far. Tucking the calculator back into her pocket, she decided she would just have to cross her fingers and hope for the best.

10

"DID YOU SEE my awesome ride?" Todd cried, almost running into Lisa as she walked out of the stable. He was leading his horse toward the water trough, and Lisa saw that there was a yellow ribbon clipped to Alamo's bridle.

"You came in third? That's great," she said, hoping she sounded enthusiastic. The truth was, she couldn't care less about Todd's ribbon in hunter jumping. All she could focus on right now was the event ahead of her. Soon it wouldn't matter that Carole and Stevie had finished ahead of her in all the other events. Soon nobody would remember that she hadn't been riding as long as her friends had. She could almost picture the blue ribbon fluttering from Major's bridle; she could almost taste the victory. And it tasted sweet—as sweet as the chocolate chip cookie she had bought and tucked into her pocket for luck. As soon as the ribbon was hers, she would eat every bite of it.

More than twenty campers had decided to enter the show-jumping event, and Lisa had drawn number seventeen. She wished she could go earlier and get it over with, but maybe it was better to go near the end. That way she would know exactly how well she had to do to win. She found a spot near the fence and settled in to watch the earlier riders take their turns.

Carole had checked Starlight's tack as soon as the hunters had finished. When he was ready to go, she left him in his stall and went outside to watch the first few riders. The crowd around the ring was bigger than ever—everyone wanted to find a spot with a good view for this event. Carole heard someone calling her name, and she turned to see Stevie, Phil, and Todd waving at her. She joined them and congratulated Todd on his ribbon, which he was wearing clipped to the neck of his shirt.

"It's a new fashion statement," he explained. "If you want people to think you're a winner, you've got to dress like one, right?"

Stevie rolled her eyes. "What number did you get?" she asked Carole.

"Five," Carole said. "How about you?"

"I got number twelve," Stevie said. She jerked a thumb at Phil. "He's seven."

Todd glanced at the ring, where the first rider was

warming up. "Look, it's your friend Melissa from the woods," he commented. The girls had told him and Phil about the couple they had mistaken for Barry.

"Very funny," Carole said. "Hey, where's Lisa? I don't think I've seen her since she finished her round in equitation."

"She's around somewhere," Todd said. "I saw her outside the stable a few minutes ago. I wonder what number she got?"

Before they could discuss it any further, the event began. Melissa and her horse, a large, muscular chestnut, started at a strong canter. The horse seemed to fly over the first obstacle with no effort at all, and the rest of the round followed suit. The pair finished with no faults.

"Wow," Phil said with a low whistle as Melissa rode out of the ring to the crowd's applause. "Talk about setting the pace. That was beautiful. If anyone else does that, it's going to mean a jump-off."

Carole felt her stomach flip with excitement. She glanced at Stevie, who looked just as thrilled.

"Fantastic," Stevie said. "The more riders in the jump-off, the more fences people have to pay for."

Carole stayed to watch the next couple of riders. Number two knocked down two rails, including a formidable-looking oxer near the end of the course. Number three rode clean but too slowly, which meant a time penalty. As the fourth rider entered the ring, Carole took a deep breath. "I'd better go get ready," she said. "Wish me luck."

Carole rode Starlight toward the ring just in time to see the rider ahead of her bring down the final rail after an otherwise clean round. The crowd groaned sympathetically, and Carole did the same. Then it was time to forget about everything else and concentrate on her own ride.

Starlight felt alert and strong under her as she entered the ring and warmed up. She nodded at Betty, who was the timekeeper for the event, and prepared to start.

When Betty gave the signal, Carole was ready, and so was Starlight. He leaped forward, breaking into a smooth, fast canter immediately. Carole aimed him at the first fence, which looked very large as they approached it. But they had practiced this often enough, and their approach was flawless. Starlight soared over the fence, and though there was no way for Carole to know for sure, she would swear that there were at least six inches of daylight between his hooves and the top rail.

He snorted a little as she brought him around and steadied him for the approach to the second fence. Carole almost laughed out loud at the sound. She could tell her horse was fired up and enjoying himself. But she forced herself to focus as they neared the obstacle, a post-and-rail fence.

The jump flew beneath them as easily as the first. So did the next one, and the in-and-out combination that

108

followed that. Even the monster oxer couldn't stop them. By the time they reached the final jump, a brush fence, Carole was grinning ear to ear. Starlight landed the last jump as perfectly as he had the first. She glanced at the clock, saw that they were within the allotted time, and let out a triumphant whoop that was loud enough to carry to where Stevie, Phil, and Todd were standing. They grinned and whooped back. Then Phil hurried off to prepare for his round.

"This means a jump-off," Todd told Stevie.

Stevie nodded. "And there are still plenty of riders to go. This is good. This is very, very good." The next rider was already entering the ring. Stevie glanced at her. "Ugh, it's that snotty girl, Arianna," she said. "Even though I can't stand her, I hope she goes clean. The more people that ride in the jump-off, the more fences you have to clear to win, and the more money we'll have when this is all over."

Stevie got her wish. Arianna rode clean. So did Phil, who went next. That meant that not only was there a jump-off, but a rider had to be in it to have any chance at one of the top ribbons.

By the time Phil finished his round, Lisa had bitten her fingernails down to the nubs. It was getting harder and harder to watch and wait and worry about how she would do when her turn came. Finally she couldn't take it anymore. She had to think about something else. As the rider after Phil brought down the top rail on the very first fence, Lisa did her best to remind herself of everything she had accomplished in the last couple of weeks. She had stayed up until almost three A.M. the night before finishing another book, so now she only had six books left to go on her reading list.

For a moment she frowned, wishing it could be fewer. Camp was ending the next day, and she wasn't going to be able to finish six more books by then. But she comforted herself with the thought that she was sticking to her diet, even though she was hungry almost all the time now. Despite how hard everything else seemed to be these days, dieting had actually turned out to be pretty easy.

Lisa hardly heard the polite applause that accompanied the rider's exit from the ring as she thought about her diet. She had stopped eating breakfast entirely, except for the sips of juice she would take whenever her friends were looking at her. At lunch and dinner, she tried not to eat more than three bites of anything, and if something looked particularly fattening, she would skip it. For instance, that day she had eaten three carrot sticks, a single spoonful of the rich beef stew, and half a piece of unbuttered toast, but she had left the chocolate pudding untouched.

The words danced in her head as she thought about them, turning into a sort of a chant: *three carrots, spoonful of stew, half a piece of toast . . . three carrots, spoonful of stew, half a piece of toast . . . three carrots, spoonful of stew, half a piece of toast . . .*

Another round of applause brought Lisa back to her senses. She shook her head to clear it, feeling annoyed with herself. She had to stay alert until it was her turn to ride. This was no time to start spacing out—she couldn't afford a mistake today.

BY THE TIME Stevie's turn came, only one more rider had made it into the jump-off. Three more had knocked down the big oxer, and the others had had other jumping or time faults. She took a deep breath and patted Belle on the neck as she waited for Betty to give the signal to start.

The first few fences were no problem. Belle seemed to understand exactly what was expected of her, and she tucked her rear hooves neatly under her as she sailed over each obstacle.

Then they approached the oxer. Belle cantered to it in perfect position, but as soon as her hooves left the ground, Stevie could feel that her horse hadn't taken off quite as powerfully as she had on the earlier fences, even though this double fence was the largest one on the course. Her heart leaped to her throat as she waited for the telltale sound of rails clattering to the ground. Instead, she heard something even more nerveracking—the sound of the mare's rear hooves scraping the top of the back rail. Stevie tensed her shoulders, waiting for the rail to fall. But after a second, the gasps of relief from the crowd told her that it had stayed in the cups. Stevie let out her own sigh of relief and did her best to maintain her focus as Belle headed for the last few fences. Even though Belle had touched the rail, it had stayed up, and that was all that counted in show jumping. They were still clean.

They stayed that way for the rest of the round. Whatever had happened at the oxer, Belle had shaken it off, and she jumped strongly over the remaining obstacles. Stevie grinned and basked in the cheers that greeted her finish, then leaned down to give Belle a fond slap on the neck. They had made it into the jump-off.

WHEN LISA ENTERED the ring, she was so nervous she could hardly stand it. Her hands were sweating, her stomach was churning, and her knees felt wobbly. Major's ears flicked back and forth at the noise from the crowd, but he didn't seem affected by the excited mood of the show.

As the gelding trotted to warm up, Lisa gripped the reins tightly and tried to think about everything she needed to know. She reviewed the order of the fences in her head: *white gate, post-and-rail, chicken coop, in-and-out* . . . When she got to the oxer, she made a mental note to be extra careful on that one—lots of riders had been knocked out of the jump-off when they had reached it.

Charlotte McNeill.

And she had to remember the time. Major was a good, steady jumper, but he wasn't particularly fast. She was going to have to keep his pace up, or they'd end up with time faults. For a second, she wished she was on Prancer, the speedy ex-racehorse she rode at Pine Hollow. But those thoughts fled when she turned Major back toward the beginning of the course and saw Betty waiting for her. It was time to start.

The first half of the course went well. Major cantered briskly between fences, not the least bit flustered by any of them. Lisa had spent an hour pacing off the course the evening before, and she knew exactly how many strides her horse needed between each jump. With her guidance, Major was able to take off smartly from just the right position every time.

As they left the sixth obstacle safely behind, Lisa started to relax just a little. For a second, she couldn't help feeling proud of the job they had done so far. And for that second, she allowed herself to think that even if they knocked down every fence from now on, she could still be satisfied with what she had accomplished—a great start in a tough event.

Then she remembered what was at stake and started to panic. She couldn't slack off now, not after she had worked so hard for this moment. This was her time to shine, to show everyone that she, Lisa Atwood, was a winner. She wasn't just Carole and Stevie's less-accomplished friend, but a great rider in her own right. To prove it, she had to win the blue ribbon. That meant no faults.

They didn't have any jumping faults so far, but what about time faults? For a moment she had forgotten all about the time. Were they cantering too slowly? Was the clock running out even now? She decided to pick up the pace and urged Major to lengthen his stride.

She had been working with him on that for weeks, and he responded immediately. Unfortunately, Lisa had forgotten to take into account the pacing to the next obstacle, a plank fence. By the time she realized it, they were only a few strides away from the jump. She frantically tried to shorten Major's stride again, but it was too late. He had to take off from too close to the fence, wasn't able to get enough height, and brought down the top two rails with his front legs. The rails clattered to the ground, and Lisa felt her mind freeze at the sound. It was the sound of her goal slipping irrevocably out of her grasp.

She hardly remembered the rest of the course, even the oxer, which came down as well. As soon as she finished her round, she dismounted and led Major back toward the stable. She had no interest in the jump-off now that she wasn't going to be in it. All she wanted to do was get away from there and be alone with her failure.

CAROLE AND STEVIE tried to find Lisa during the break before the jump-off.

"She's got to be around here someplace," Carole said. "I'm sure she wouldn't miss the jump-off." Several members of the staff were in the ring, entertaining the audience with an amateur rodeo-clown show. The jump-off was scheduled to start in twenty minutes.

Stevie shrugged. "Who can find anyone in this crowd?" she said, proudly surveying the happy spectators all around them. Just then she spotted the red-haired woman she had met in town. The woman was holding her baby in one arm and had the other wrapped around a tall, thin man. Stevie smiled. The couple appeared to be reliving some romantic memories, and who could blame them? This was the perfect place for it.

That reminded her to look around for Phil. Just because they were going to compete against each other in the jump-off in a few minutes, it didn't mean this wasn't the perfect time for a little romantic rendezvous of their own.

SIX COMPETITORS HAD made it into the jump-off. This time they only had to jump six fences instead of twelve, but the time allowance had been slashed by more than half, so it was going to be a real challenge to avoid time faults.

The riders drew new numbers, and Phil went first. His horse, Teddy, raced through the course at a scorching pace, but they ended up paying for his speed with mistakes. The pair finished within the allotted time but with two fences down.

The spectators were on the edge of their seats as the other riders competed one by one. Melissa had a two-second time fault and one rail down. Stevie finished just a hair under the deadline, but she, too, brought down a fence. The next two riders couldn't seem to decide whether to be cautious or fast. They both had time and multiple jumping faults.

At last it was Carole's turn. She liked going last, because she knew exactly what she had to do to win. "Okay, boy," she murmured to Starlight as they warmed up. "We're a team, right? We know we can do this, because we're doing it together. Just remember—slow and steady wins the race."

Realizing that every other rider had at least one jumping fault—which counted much more heavily against them than time faults—Carole had decided to forget about the time and ride at a comfortable pace. If they could jump every obstacle cleanly, they should be able to win even with several time faults.

Starlight did his part, and the rails stayed up. It wasn't a perfect round, because he and Carole did have several seconds' worth of time faults. But it was good enough to win the blue ribbon. The crowd stood and applauded wildly as Barry announced the results. Stevie and Belle had come in a close second, and Melissa and her horse took third.

Carole and Stevie dismounted and hugged each other, grinning wildly. Then they waited as Barry announced the rest of the winners, cheering loudly for their other friends. Phil had come in fourth, and Lisa ended up winning the light blue ribbon for tenth place.

"Wow, that's pretty good, considering we weren't even sure she should have entered," Carole commented. "She should be proud of that."

Stevie nodded in agreement. But Lisa didn't come forward to claim her prize, and Barry called her name again. There was still no sign of her.

"Lisa? Are you here? I guess not," the camp director said. "Stevie, will you see that she gets this?"

"Sure." Stevie took the ribbon and glanced at Carole. "Where do you think she is?" she whispered.

Carole shrugged. "She could be inside with Major." But she wasn't convinced, and she knew Stevie wasn't, either.

Soon the awards ceremony was finished. The show was over. As the happy spectators began drifting back to their cars, the jump-off competitors led their tired horses into the stable for a well-deserved rest. Carole and Stevie made sure that Starlight and Belle were comfortable, then gave their tack a quick cleaning. Lisa hadn't turned up by the time they had finished, so they searched the stable for her. She was nowhere to be found, so they hurried back to their cabin. It was empty.

"Where could she be?" Stevie said. "Do you think we just missed her in the crowd?" A lot of people had left, but there were quite a few stragglers talking to the campers about the show and buying the last of the cookies and lemonade. Even though Carole and Stevie had loved every second of the show, it was a relief to get away from the meadow to the relative peace of the cabin area.

"It's possible," Carole said. "But I doubt it. I don't remember seeing her around the show grounds after her last round. Do you think she could be down at the pond?"

"There's only one way to find out."

The girls left their cabin and made their way carefully down the narrow, twisting path from the cabins to the pond. When they were almost there, they heard voices.

"That sounds like Barry," Carole said quietly. "What's he doing down here?"

"Let's find out," Stevie whispered back. The two girls stayed silent, trying to hear what Barry was saying.

"We've had one heck of a great time here over the years, haven't we?" he said, his voice sounding happy and sad at the same time.

"That's for sure." The girls recognized Betty's voice. "I can't believe it's all about to end. But at least we went out with a bang. Can you believe how many people turned out for the show?"

"I know, it's unbelievable, isn't it?" Barry replied. "I'm glad we did the show jumping—that was a great idea."

"Thanks," Betty said. "So was your idea for this month-long session."

The girls heard Barry sigh. "Yeah, this summer was

pretty great overall, despite a few sour notes here and there."

"You mean like bulldozers lurking in the woods?" Betty asked.

Barry chuckled. "Actually, I was thinking about some other things. Like our poor little friend, Miss Sullivan."

Carole almost gasped out loud. Barry was talking about Piper!

"That whole situation is really sad," Betty said. "It sounds like they got her to the hospital just in time. I only hope they can help her."

Carole and Stevie exchanged wide-eyed glances, waiting for the adults to go on. But Barry changed the subject, talking about a horse with a swollen ankle and a couple of other minor problems that had cropped up during the month. When the girls were sure they weren't going to hear anything else of importance, they turned and quietly crept back toward the cabins.

"How about that?" Stevie said. "Piper's in the hospital. I wonder what's wrong with her?"

"I don't know," Carole replied. "And I don't think we should mention this to Lisa until we find out. It would only worry her more." She didn't say so, but she was thinking about Betty's last words: *I only hope they can help her*. That didn't sound good.

"Agreed," Stevie replied. She clambered up the last few feet of the path, emerging in front of their cabin just in time to see Lisa jogging toward them, wearing shorts and sneakers. Her face was red with exertion, and her T-shirt was wet with sweat.

"There you are!" Carole cried. "Where have you been?"

Lisa seemed startled to see them. "Oh, uh, I just went for a quick run," she said breathlessly. "Is the show over?"

"I thought you hated jogging," Stevie said.

Lisa shrugged. "I used to," she said quickly. "But my ballet teacher is always bugging me to stay in shape, so I figured I'd give it a try."

Carole frowned. Lisa's ballet teacher had been trying to get her to jog for years, and Lisa had always laughed it off before. Why would she suddenly decide to start jogging now—especially in the middle of a horse show? This was getting stranger all the time. And the longer Lisa's odd behavior continued, the harder it was for Carole to believe it would go away on its own.

"Stevie! Hey, Stevie!" called an excited voice. Several campers were hurrying toward them, waving their sponsor sheets. With that, Lisa's jogging was forgotten—at least for the moment. For the next hour or two, campers turned up in a steady stream to drop off their sponsor sheets. Most of them hung around to talk about the show or to see how much money they had raised.

Stevie and her calculator stayed busy adding up the numbers as they came in. One of the volunteer ticket sellers showed up to report the take at the gate, and the dressage instructor, who had been manning the refreshment table, came by with her numbers as well. Last but not least, Mike knocked on the door. He had just spent the last hour on the phone with parents and had an early estimate for the videotape sales.

Taken separately, the numbers all seemed impressive. But before the evening was over, Stevie discovered to her dismay that no matter how many times she added them up, the total just wasn't enough. They were still almost ten thousand dollars short.

THE FINAL DAY of camp was a gloomy one. That had nothing to do with the weather—it was a perfect summer Saturday—and everything to do with the mood of the campers when they learned that Moose Hill was doomed despite everything they had done.

After breakfast, Stevie decided it was time to tell Barry everything. She found Carole and Lisa in the cabin. Lisa was reading *Hamlet*, and Carole was packing. Both of them seemed a little distracted when Stevie told them what she planned to do, but both agreed to come along.

Barry's jaw dropped when he heard about the fundraiser. For a moment he seemed unable to speak. "You—you mean you kids raised more than twenty thousand dollars just from the horse show yesterday?" he stammered at last.

Stevie nodded. "The only problem was, we needed to raise *thirty* thousand."

Barry ran one hand through his hair. He couldn't seem to decide whether to smile or frown. "I can't believe it," he said, finally settling on a smile. "This was all supposed to be a secret, but—well, thanks, girls. Thanks a lot. I really appreciate your efforts—it's good to know that this place means so much to someone besides me." He sighed. "Actually, though, I guess I should tell you that even the thirty thousand I mentioned was a rounded-off number. The amount I needed was more like thirty-four thousand."

For some reason, that made Stevie feel even worse. She handed Barry the envelope she was holding. "Here's the money we collected so far. I guess we should give it all back."

"Not necessarily," Barry said. "Let me talk to some of the people in town and figure out an appropriate charity to donate it to."

The Saddle Club just nodded. They were glad the money they had raised would be going to a good cause, but they couldn't work up much enthusiasm at the thought. It wouldn't be the cause they had wanted.

Barry tucked the envelope in his desk drawer. "I might as well tell you the rest of the bad news," he said quietly.

"I spoke with Fred Winter a few minutes ago. He tells me they're close to finalizing the deal and are expecting to sign the papers first thing Monday morning."

"Then those bulldozers will be able to get right to work," Lisa said grimly. Even though she hadn't been giving her full attention to the efforts to save Moose Hill, she was sorry that the plan had failed. But it fit right in with her own morose mood since losing the show-jumping competition. During her jog the day before, she had thrown the chocolate chip cookie she had bought as far into the woods as she could. Even if she couldn't do anything else right, there was still one thing she could do, and that was stick to her diet.

Barry sighed. "I still can't quite believe this is happening," he said, his voice so sad that the girls could hardly stand it. "This place has been my home for the past ten years—the people here have been my family. And Monday morning it will all be over."

After that, there didn't seem to be much left to say. The girls left Barry's office and wandered out into the bright morning sunshine.

"It seems like it should be raining," Carole said gloomily.

Stevie shrugged. "Well, it's not," she said. "Anybody want to go for one last trail ride or something?"

"I'm not in the mood," Carole said. Now that they had wrapped things up with Barry, she was starting to think more seriously about Lisa's problem. "Besides, I already put on Starlight's traveling bandages."

"Oh, right," Stevie said. "I did Belle's, too." She fell silent for a moment. "Still, I'd really like to ride out into the woods once more," she said at last. "Maybe even take another look at those bulldozers."

"Why?" Lisa asked.

"I don't know," Stevie replied. "I just feel like I need to see them one more time to really convince myself that our plan failed." The word tasted bad as it left her mouth. The Saddle Club had never failed at something this important before.

Lisa was nodding, looking thoughtful. "Believe it or not, that actually makes sense," she said. "I'd come with you, except I really want to do some reading . . ."

"Forget about that for once, will you?" Stevie snapped. "It's the last day at camp. You can read all the way home in the van if you want to. But please come along now, okay?"

Lisa looked uncertain, but finally she nodded. "Okay."

"You two go ahead," Carole said. "I'm going to stay here."

Stevie gave her a surprised look and opened her mouth to argue.

Carole cut her off before she could say a word. "I mean it," she said. "There's something I have to do before we leave."

Stevie gave in with a shrug. "Why don't we both ride Major," she said to Lisa. "That way I won't have to redo Belle's bandages."

As soon as her friends had disappeared into the barn, Carole began searching for Betty. She was determined to find out the whole story of what had happened to Piper. Since Barry had made it clear that he wasn't going to tell her anything, she would ask Betty. And this time she wasn't going to take "none of your business" for an answer.

Carole found Betty in one of the sheds. The instructor was making a list of the equipment there, adding notes about what would happen to it when the camp closed.

"It's not a very fun task," she told Carole. "But I could use some help if you've got a few minutes."

"Sure," Carole said. She took the paper and pencil Betty handed her and began digging through one of the toolboxes, writing down the names of the items she found there. After working in silence for a moment, she cleared her throat. "Betty," she said. "There's something I have to ask you."

"I hope it's not about what I'm going to do with myself starting Monday," Betty said. "Because I have no idea. None of us does, really."

Carole shook her head. "That's not it," she said as she dropped a pair of pliers back into the box. "It has nothing to do with Moose Hill's closing."

Betty looked surprised. "Ask away, then."

"It's about Piper," Carole began. "I need to know what happened to her."

Betty looked even more surprised, as well as a little cautious. "I'm not sure why you're asking, but I really think Barry's the one you should talk to about this. All I know is that she had to leave for personal reasons."

"I know that's not true." Normally Carole would never have the guts to say such a thing to an adult, but she was getting desperate. She couldn't help thinking that Lisa's peace of mind was depending on her. "I overheard you and Barry talking about it last night by the pond. You said she was in the hospital. I'm sorry for eavesdropping, but I know you know what happened to her, and I've really got to find out the truth. For Lisa's sake."

"Lisa? What does she have to do with this?" Betty asked quickly. "I know they were cabin mates, but—"

"Lisa hasn't been the same since Piper disappeared," Carole replied. "Her whole personality has changed. She barely sleeps, she skips half her meals, and she never seems to smile anymore." Carole didn't realize how true the last part was until she said it. Lisa had the kind of smile that brought her whole face to life, and Carole hadn't seen it in far too long.

Betty's shoulders sagged. "Oh, no," she said, sinking down onto a pile of empty feed sacks. "It can't be."

Her face had gone pale, and Carole felt frightened, though she wasn't sure why. "What?" she whispered. "Please, you have to tell me."

"I guess I do," Betty said. She took a deep breath. "Carole, have you ever heard of a disease called anorexia nervosa?"

Carole nodded. "We studied it in health class last year. It's when people starve themselves to lose weight."

"That's right," Betty said. "But there's more to it than that. It's an eating disorder, but it's really about more than losing weight. It seems to be mostly about being in control. And it's all too common among teenage girls who seem to have everything going for them. Girls like Piper."

"You mean Piper has anorexia?" The thought made Carole go cold all over. Piper had seemed so perfect, so smart and successful. And Carole's health teacher had told the class that some victims of anorexia got so sick that they eventually died. Carole set down the list she had been making and sat down next to Betty. "I can't believe it. She was thin, but she didn't look sick."

Betty sighed. "I know it isn't easy to believe, but I'm afraid it's true. Piper has been struggling with anorexia for years. In the past year she seemed to finally be getting over it for good, and that's why her parents decided to let her come to camp. But once she arrived, she stopped eating again. Fortunately her parents had told Barry

128

about her history, and as soon as he realized what was happening he called them. It took him a while to catch on, though—Piper has had anorexia for so long that she's become an expert at hiding her problem from the people around her."

"I still can't believe it," Carole said, shaking her head. "She seemed so normal. Well, better than normal, actually. She's a fantastic rider." But even as she said it, she remembered that Piper had rarely come to meals, and she had eaten very little when she had. Also, she had exercised almost nonstop—if she wasn't riding, she was swimming or jogging or playing tennis.

"I know," Betty said, nodding. "She was one of the best riders at camp because she liked to succeed. But anorexics often feel such a driving need to succeed, to control their own lives, that they feel they must control every bite that enters their mouth. Their need to be thin sort of takes over their mind, and they'll do anything to lose just one more pound."

Carole felt bad for Piper, but she was even more worried about Lisa. "Could—Could Lisa's weird behavior mean that living with Piper made her get anorexia?"

"Anorexia isn't contagious the way the flu or measles is," Betty said. She gave Carole a searching look. "But if Lisa is acting as oddly as you say, I suppose it's possible that Piper's behavior somehow influenced her own. I'm no expert, though. If you're really worried, you have to see that she gets professional help."

"I don't know . . ." Carole thought hard for a moment. Piper had obviously had a strong effect on Lisa, and not necessarily a good one. But maybe all Lisa needed was to find out what had happened to her friend. Once she realized what she was doing, she would stop—she was too sensible not to. Once camp was over, maybe all of them, including Lisa, could put this behind them.

"I'll speak to Barry about Lisa if you like," Betty offered. "Or if you'd rather he didn't know, I could call Lisa's parents and talk to them about it."

Carole stood up and rubbed her forehead. This was too much for her to take in all at once. Lisa really did seem to be in some kind of trouble, but Carole wasn't sure that calling in the adults was the right thing to do. Somehow, that seemed like a betrayal of everything The Saddle Club stood for. If Lisa's problems didn't go away on their own once they left camp, maybe Carole and Stevie could figure out a way to help her. "Don't do anything yet, okay?" she said. "Let me think about it first."

Betty nodded reluctantly. "Please let me know what you decide," she said. "If Lisa's in the kind of trouble you're afraid of, she needs help fast."

MEANWHILE LISA AND Stevie were riding bareback through the forest toward the spot where the bulldozers had been heading. They didn't talk much as they rode, letting Major choose his own pace along the sun-dappled trails.

130

As they neared their goal, the sound of motors came to them. "What do you think they're doing?" Stevie asked in surprise. She had expected the machinery to be waiting silently for Monday morning, when it could begin chewing its way through the forest.

Lisa just shrugged. "There's only one way to find out."

The girls rode toward the noise. The closer they got, the louder it was. "It's a good thing we're both riding Major," Stevie said. "There's no way Belle would get this close to that kind of racket."

Finally they came upon the same caravan of machinery they had seen before. Once again, the giant machines were on the move, crawling along the wide dirt road through the forest. Stevie urged Major forward, and the horse stepped out onto the road ahead of the first bulldozer.

The same man, Bill, was driving. He frowned when he saw the horse and cut the motor. "You again?" he said, recognizing Stevie. He didn't sound very happy to see her.

"Me again," Stevie replied grimly. "Where are you guys going this time? I thought you weren't supposed to start work until next week."

"Tell me about it," Bill said, looking disgruntled. The other machines had stopped and were idling behind him. "Believe me, it wasn't my choice to work on a Saturday. But we've got orders to take the equipment to the edge of the woods." He jerked his chin in the direction of camp.

"Apparently there's some kind of pond down there that needs to be filled in first thing."

Stevie and Lisa gasped in horror. The swimming pond! "But why would they want to get rid of the pond?" Lisa cried. Would nothing be spared?

Bill shrugged. "Don't ask me," he said brusquely. "I just follow orders. Now if you'll get that beast of yours out of the road, we'll be on our way. There's a game on TV in a couple of hours, and I'd like to be home to see it."

Stevie shook her head. "Sorry," she said, not sounding sorry at all. "I'm afraid we can't do that."

The worker looked almost as surprised as Lisa felt at Stevie's words. "No joking around now, kids," he said. "We've got work to do."

"You can do it on Monday when the papers are signed," Stevie said. She slid down from Major's back and stood in the road in front of the big machine, her hands on her hips. "Until then, Moose Hill still belongs to us. And we don't want your horrible machines lurking around our swimming pond." To everyone's amazement, she lay down in the dusty road in front of the bulldozer's wheels.

Bill just rolled his eyes and started the motor. Lisa gasped, horrified, but Bill turned the wheel sharply, moving carefully around Stevie's prostrate form. The rest of the drivers threw their vehicles into gear, preparing to follow.

As soon as Stevie realized what was happening, she leaped to her feet. "We've got to stop them!" she cried to Lisa over the roar of the motors. Even steady, fearless Major was beginning to look nervous at the noise, but Stevie hardly noticed. Suddenly it seemed very important to stop this. This might be the last day of existence for Moose Hill Riding Camp, and Stevie thought the camp should be allowed to pass that day in peace, without greedy machines threatening its best places.

Lisa wasn't sure what they were supposed to do. There were only two of them, and they weren't going to be able to keep Major there much longer. Besides, even if they managed to block the road, the heavy machines could crash their way around them through the underbrush. It seemed hopeless.

But Stevie wasn't giving up this time. She hadn't been able to save Moose Hill from being sold, and that made it seem even more important to do this. "Help me up," she called, stretching her arms up over Major's back. Once Lisa had hauled her aboard, Stevie turned the horse back toward camp. "We'll be back!" she yelled at the workmen as Major cantered away.

Moments later Stevie was racing around camp, rounding up all the campers she could find and sending them running into the woods toward the construction workers. A few kids had already left, but most of those who remained were eager to join Stevie's impromptu protest.

Stevie was about to head back into the woods herself when she ran into Lisa coming out of the stable. "Have you seen Carole?" Stevie asked her.

Lisa shook her head. "Not since we got back."

"Well, there's no time to look for her now," Stevie said breathlessly. She grabbed Lisa's hand and dragged her toward the woods. "Too bad—she'll be sorry she missed this. Come on, let's get back out there!"

AT THAT MOMENT Carole was sitting in a quiet spot behind the mess hall, picking at the overgrown grass next to the building and thinking hard. She was completely unaware of the hubbub around camp that Stevie had started, because she had been in this very spot since leaving Betty.

She was doing her best to figure out what to do about Lisa, but for some reason the failed fund-raiser kept getting mixed up in her thoughts. Carole had always thought that almost any problem could be solved if you had good friends helping you. That was the idea behind the Saddle Club rule about members helping each other. This time it hadn't worked for Moose Hill, and Carole was beginning to wonder if it would work any better for Lisa.

As much as she hated to admit it, Carole was beginning to think that Lisa's problem might be too big for The Saddle Club to handle. The camp problem had been, too, but she had no regrets about their attempt to fix that. They had taken their best shot, and though they hadn't succeeded in the end, there was no harm done. As she thought about what Betty had told her about anorexia, though, Carole feared that if she and Stevie tried and failed to solve Lisa's problem, they might actually make things worse. The Moose Hill sale had been intimidating because of the huge amount of money involved. But money was just money. Lisa's health might be at stake, and that was much more intimidating than the other problem could ever have been, even if they had needed to raise thirty million dollars instead of thirty thousand.

Carole stretched out on the grass, trying to figure out what to do. If she gave up before even trying to help Lisa through whatever she was going through, did that make her a bad friend? And if Lisa's closest friends couldn't help her, who could?

Suddenly Carole sat bolt upright. One part of her mind had just accepted what she had to do to be a real friend to Lisa—make sure she talked to a professional, as Betty had suggested. But another part had just realized what she could still do to save Moose Hill. It wasn't too late. She jumped to her feet and ran toward the equipment shed as fast as she could.

BY THE TIME the protesters returned to camp, it was all settled. Stevie, Lisa, Phil, and Todd came out of the woods together.

"Did you see the look on that guy's face when those girls joined hands and made a circle around his bulldozer and started singing 'We Shall Overcome'?" Phil asked Stevie with a grin.

Stevie nodded, feeling tired but oddly triumphant. They had done what they could. They had stopped the interlopers—for the day, at least. The construction workers had done their best to resist the protesters. But after more than a dozen campers had started swarming around them, they had had no choice but to give up, and they had done so with rather bad grace, stomping off toward the main road and muttering about calling their union.

"Stevie!" a voice called. Stevie looked up and saw Carole running toward her with a big grin on her face.

"Where were you?" Stevie asked. "You missed all the excitement."

Carole's grin got even broader. "Correction," she said. "*You* missed the excitement. Moose Hill is saved!"

Stevie narrowed her eyes and stared at her friend. "You're talking about the construction workers, right?" she said.

"What construction workers?" Carole asked. She didn't bother to wait for an answer, but went on, almost dancing with her eagerness to share the news. "No, I'm talking about the camp. Barry is buying it after all. He already talked to the Winters, and it's all settled."

Stevie and the others gasped, and everyone began talking at once, trying to find out what had happened.

Carole laughed and held up her hands for silence. "It's

true," she said. "Although I wasn't being quite accurate when I said Barry is buying Moose Hill. I should have said Barry and his partners are buying it."

"His partners?" Lisa said. "What are you talking about?"

For a second Carole's grin wavered as she looked at Lisa and thought about what they still had to do to help her. But there would be time for that soon enough. "You know how Barry was always saying that the people who worked here were such good friends—like a big family?" she said. "Well, I started thinking about that. When something goes wrong, who do you turn to? Your family and friends, right?"

The others nodded, waiting for her to go on.

"Well, I was sort of thinking about that kind of thing," Carole said. She didn't plan to explain why she had been thinking that, at least not until she, Stevie, and Lisa were alone. "And for some reason I suddenly remembered how Mike the stable hand had donated his whole savings account to the cause. Then it all seemed so simple. Lots of people love Moose Hill just as much as Barry. Why shouldn't they all join forces—and buy it and run it as a team?"

Stevie slapped her forehead. Carole was right. The answer now seemed so obvious it was almost painful. "I can't believe I didn't think of that before now!" she exclaimed. "I've been racking my brains to come up with a way to raise money, and the answer was right here in front of me all along. It's perfect. Carole, you're brilliant!"

Carole smiled modestly. "I don't know about that," she said. "Even though I was the one to put two and two together, I prefer to think of it as a team effort."

Stevie grinned. "I'll buy that," she said, and everyone laughed. "So it's really all settled? Moose Hill is safe?"

"Absolutely," Carole said. "Even though Barry and his partners won't be able to pay up front like the developers, they're working out a deal with the Winters. It turns out Barry was right when he said they'd rather see this place stay a camp." She shrugged. "But the bottom line is, Team Barry has more than enough money now. Enough of the other employees are interested—including Betty and the cook and a whole bunch of others—that they hardly even need the money we raised with our fund-raiser."

Todd rubbed his hands together eagerly. "Does that mean he's giving it back to us? I could use a new skateboard."

Phil laughed and shoved his friend playfully. "Aren't three skateboards enough for you?"

"Three?" Todd said. "No way. I only brought three to camp, but I have four more back home."

Carole waited for them to stop clowning around, then answered Todd's question. "Actually, the money will come in handy," she said. "Even though they don't need it to buy the camp, they're going to need it for expenses in running it until money starts coming in."

"That won't take long," Stevie predicted confidently. "Once Barry and his team are in charge of this place, it will be even more wonderful than it was before. They'll be turning people away."

"Just as long as they don't turn *us* away," Phil joked.

Stevie, Carole, and Lisa exchanged smiles. "Don't worry, he wouldn't dare," Stevie said. "We're all part of his team."

THE HOUR WAS approaching when Red was due to pick up The Saddle Club and take them home. They were ready—almost. Carole waited until Lisa was busy packing and then dragged Stevie away for a serious talk. She told her what Betty had said and convinced her of what they had to do.

Carole and Stevie shook hands solemnly, then went back into the cabin to talk to Lisa. Luckily, their other cabin mates weren't there.

"Lisa, sit down for a minute, please," Carole said. "We have something to say to you."

Lisa glanced up from her packing, startled by her friend's serious tone. "What's the matter?"

"Just sit down, okay?" Stevie said.

Lisa dropped the shirt she had been folding and perched on the edge of her bunk, looking confused.

Carole took a deep breath. "Lisa, we found out what happened to Piper."

For a second Lisa's eyes lit up. "You did?" Then she realized that Carole and Stevie still looked somber. "What happened? Was it something bad? Tell me!"

"We're not going to lie," Stevie said. "It *was* something bad. Piper has anorexia." As soon as she had learned why Piper had left, a lot of things Stevie had noticed about Lisa's cabin mate had fallen into place. One of the older girls at Stevie's school was anorexic, and now Stevie could see some similarities between her and Piper.

Lisa just looked puzzled. "What?" she said. "That's crazy. Piper didn't have anything like that wrong with her. She was perfectly normal."

"No, she wasn't," Stevie said firmly. "And you haven't been acting normal lately, either. We think you might be developing the same kind of problem."

"That's right," Carole put in, trying to keep her voice from shaking. She reminded herself that this was for Lisa's own good. "Piper is sick, and we don't want you to end up like her."

Lisa gave a short laugh. "I can think of a lot of worse things than ending up like Piper," she said. "I don't know why you guys have suddenly decided you don't like her, but I don't appreciate this one bit."

"We don't care if you appreciate it or not," Stevie said firmly. "Piper's in the hospital. You've been hurting yourself for weeks now, and we can't just sit back and let you keep doing it. We're going to help you whether you want us to or not, and that means convincing you to talk to a professional about your problem."

"I don't have a problem!" Lisa snapped. "The only ones with problems around here are you two, so just go away and leave me alone, okay?"

Carole shook her head sadly. She glanced at the bag of books lying on the floor near Lisa's bunk. "We've been leaving you alone for too long already. You're pushing yourself too hard. You read all the time, and when you're not doing that, you're practicing your riding."

"That's over now," Lisa muttered, shrugging. "I already lost the show. Another failure."

"What do you mean?" Stevie asked.

Lisa shrugged again, still looking angry. "First that B-plus, then my reading list, then the show. It seems like everything I do these days is a big failure."

"Is that why you started skipping meals?" Carole asked, remembering what Betty had said. "Because your eating was something you could control?"

Lisa looked wary. "What do you mean?" she said. "I don't really skip meals. I just don't always eat them in the mess hall."

"Don't lie to us, Lisa," Carole said sadly. "I checked with Barry's assistant. He sits right across the hall from those snack machines you were talking about before, and he said he hasn't seen you there even once."

Lisa's face crumpled. "Don't you trust me?" she asked, her voice wavering. "I thought you were supposed to be my best friends."

"We are," Stevie replied. "That's why we're going to tell your parents about this if you won't. Even if it means you never speak to us again."

Lisa glanced at Carole, who was nodding at what Stevie had said. "Why are you doing this to me?" she whispered.

Carole couldn't meet her eyes. "We want you to go back to how you used to be," she said. "We want you to get better."

Lisa continued to argue for a few more minutes, but finally she seemed to give up. "Okay, maybe things have gotten a little out of control lately," she said. "There was just so much to do, you know?" She sighed. "Do you know how Piper is? I mean, how sick is she?"

"I'm not sure," Carole said. "She's in the hospital. Maybe you can write to her there or something."

Lisa nodded and leaned back against the wall behind her bunk. "It's so weird how things turn out sometimes," she said. "I wanted to be more like her, and I guess I might have succeeded a little too well. But I also wanted to be more like you, and I didn't have much luck with that at all."

"What do you mean?" Stevie asked.

"You two are such great riders," Lisa replied. "Everyone

says so. I'll never be able to catch up, no matter how hard I work. It just doesn't seem fair that you'll always know more than I do."

Carole could see Lisa's point. "I guess that's one way to look at it," she said. "But it's not easy the other way around, either. When everyone expects you to be the best every time, that can put a lot of pressure on you."

"Right," Stevie said, leaning against the cabin wall. "Besides, there are some advantages for you, too. You get the benefit of all our hard-won knowledge because we're friends."

"We *are* still friends, aren't we?" Carole asked softly.

Lisa nodded and smiled a little, feeling slightly comforted by her friends' words. "We're still friends," she said. "But as my friends, I hope you don't mean it about telling my parents. Maybe I have been working a little too hard lately, but I can deal with it myself. Really."

"Sorry," Stevie said. "We can't do that."

Lisa frowned. "Come on," she said. "Things aren't that bad. I just have to lighten up a little, and everything will be fine."

Carole shook her head. "I don't think so," she said. "When you're lying to your two best friends, things have already gone too far."

Lisa started to respond, then stopped herself. She thought about what Carole had said, and suddenly she realized it was true. "All right," she said after a long pause.

"You win. Maybe it wouldn't hurt for me to talk to some-one."

Carole and Stevie heaved a joint sigh of relief and sat down on either side of Lisa to give her a big three-way hug. This time they knew she wasn't lying to them. She had taken a big, difficult first step, and they were going to stick with her every step of the way. That was what friends were for.

A LITTLE OVER A month later, Carole and Stevie were in the student locker room at Pine Hollow, getting ready to go on a trail ride.

"What time is Lisa getting here?" Stevie asked as she pulled on her boots.

Carole glanced at her watch. "She should be here any minute now," she replied. "She had another appointment with Susan, and she was going to come here straight from that."

Stevie nodded. Lisa had been seeing a teen counselor since arriving home from camp. At first it hadn't been easy for her to talk to a stranger about her feelings, but lately she had told her friends that things were going much better.

At that moment Lisa herself walked into the room. "There you are," she said. "I was afraid you'd left without me."

"Never," Stevie declared. "How was your appoint-ment?"

"Great," Lisa said with a smile. "Susan thinks I've made lots of progress in the past couple of weeks."

"That's fantastic!" Stevie said.

Carole reached out to give Lisa a hug. "We're really proud of you."

"Thanks." Lisa tossed her sneakers into her cubby and took out her riding boots. "But you guys deserve some of the credit, too, you know. Susan says the main reason I'm doing so well is that I got help so quickly. If you two hadn't figured out what was going on and forced me to face it, I might have been in a lot of trouble by now."

Carole and Stevie nodded. They already knew that Lisa was lucky she had gotten help before her early symptoms had turned into a full-fledged eating disorder such as anorexia. A lot of girls weren't so lucky.

"That's what we're here for," Carole said. "You'd do the same for either of us, right?"

Lisa nodded as the girls left the locker area and headed for the tack room. "We make a pretty good team, don't we?" she mused. "I think that's another part of the reason I'm going to be okay." Susan had told her that having such supportive friends and a loving family was probably the reason she hadn't had problems before this, despite the high standards she always set for herself. In addition to the support she got from the other members of The Saddle Club, Lisa had rediscovered how deeply her parents cared about her. They were very involved in their daughter's therapy sessions, and the family had become a lot closer as a result.

"We *do* make a good team," Stevie said. "And you'd better not forget it again. Remember, we're here to help each other—if any of us ever feels overwhelmed by things, we've got to talk to each other."

Lisa smiled. "I know that now. I don't suppose I'll ever be happy with anything less than straight As or blue ribbons, but thanks to Susan I'm finally learning how to handle it better when I don't get them."

"Nobody's perfect," Carole said, nodding. Then she grinned. "Although I think the three of us come pretty close sometimes."

"Only when we're working as a team," Lisa said. Her smile faded. "I just hope I can be of some help to Piper, like you guys are for me." She had found a letter from Piper waiting for her when she had arrived home from camp, and the two girls had been writing to each other ever since. Piper's latest letter had arrived the day before. Unfortunately Piper's recovery wasn't nearly as assured as Lisa's own. She had been struggling with her disease for a long time and had had many setbacks. Several times before this, her parents had thought she was finally cured—in fact, Piper's horse, Tapestry, had been a gift during one of those times—only to have her fall back into her old patterns once again. But she was trying, and Lisa hoped that this time her new friend would defeat the disease once and for all. Until she did, all Lisa could do to help her was to keep writing, and to let her know she had at least one friend who cared about her even if she wasn't perfect.

She told her friends what she was thinking as they picked up their horses' tack. "I know it probably won't happen, but I can't help hoping she'll be better in time to come to Moose Hill again next summer."

Carole nodded sympathetically. "You never know. Miracles do happen sometimes."

"They sure do," Stevie said, slinging Belle's bridle over one shoulder. "After all, even the fact that Moose Hill will be around next summer is practically a miracle."

"A Saddle Club miracle," Carole agreed with a grin. "That's the best kind." The girls had heard that Barry was already putting some of his ideas for the camp into effect. And his new partners had contributed some great ideas of their own, which made Barry even more certain that the new and improved Moose Hill Riding Camp would be a big success when it reopened for business the next summer.

"It sure is," Lisa said.

Stevie gave her a sly look. "I wonder if another certain someone will be back at camp next summer?" she commented teasingly.

"You mean Todd?" Lisa asked with a laugh. "You never give up, do you?"

Stevie shrugged. "Hey, you never know," she said.

"Maybe next year, when you're not distracted by all that other stuff—"

"I don't think so," Lisa interrupted her. "I hate to disappoint you, but even if I'd been totally my normal self this year, I still wouldn't have wanted to date Todd. He's nice and everything, but I could never go out with someone who's more interested in his skateboard than he ever could be in me."

Carole laughed and hoisted Starlight's saddle off its rack. "Too bad, Stevie," she said. "I guess you'll have to give up on finding Todd a girlfriend."

Stevie gave her a thoughtful look. "Maybe not," she said slowly. "*You* seemed to get along with him pretty well, Carole."

Carole laughed again, and Lisa joined in. Stevie would never change, and they were both glad about that. "Put it this way," Carole said. "I can't wait to see *all* our riding camp friends again next summer. You can make of that what you will, Stevie."

Lisa picked up Prancer's saddle and bridle and followed her friends out of the tack room. "Whatever else happens, I can guarantee one thing about the new and improved Moose Hill," she said.

"What's that?" Stevie and Carole asked in one voice.

Lisa smiled. "Next year, Barry will *definitely* make sure the three of us end up in the same cabin!"

About the Author

BONNIE BRYANT is the author of many books for young readers, including novelizations of movie hits such as *Teenage Mutant Ninja Turtles* and *Honey, I Blew Up the Kid*, written under her married name, B. B. Hiller.

Ms. Bryant began writing The Saddle Club in 1986. Although she had done some riding before that, she intensified her studies then and found herself learning right along with her characters Stevie, Carole, and Lisa. She claims that they are all much better riders than she is.

Ms. Bryant was born and raised in New York City. She still lives there, in Greenwich Village, with her two sons.

Did you read Bonnie Bryant's exciting companion to
Summer Rider? *Look for it in your*
favorite bookstore.

SUMMER HORSE
Saddle Club 67

The Saddle Club girls are at one of their favorite places—
Moose Hill Summer Camp. This time they're staying for
an entire month. But right away, they start to wonder if
their dream summer will be all they hoped. Lisa Atwood
learns she's in a different cabin than her best friends,
Stevie Lake and Carole Hanson. Stevie's boyfriend is
practically ignoring her. Worst of all, Carole has been
assigned a camp horse that won't cooperate. Whoever
would have thought that horse-crazy Carole would meet
an equine she can't stand!

Finally, something isn't right at Moose Hill Camp. The
camp director is acting strangely; a camper disappears; and
who owns the black limousine they keep seeing around
the camp? Can The Saddle Club find out what is going on
before it's too late?

PONY TAILS
by Bonnie Bryant

Saddle up for fun and adventure with three pony-crazy younger riders at Pine Hollow in this terrific companion series to *The Saddle Club*. May, Jasmine and Corey are three girls with a passion for ponies – and their very own club, the Pony Tails.

Available now: